'I'm spoilt?'

Kate spoke through gritted teeth, hurt that Sebastian should see her needs so easily filled by material wealth. Her father had given her everything but love.

'That's right.'

'I had everything, did I? Everything money could buy——'

Sebastian stopped her. 'We're not playing the role of poor little rich girl, are we, Kate?'

'I only ever wanted one thing, Sebastian, and you took that,' she told him, her eyes fixed on his in confrontation. 'You robbed me of my partnership in my father's company.'

Catherine O'Connor was born and has lived all her life in Manchester, where she is a happily married woman with five demanding children, a neurotic cat, an untrainable dog and a rabbit. She spends most of her time either writing or planning her next story, and without the support and encouragement of her long-suffering husband this would be impossible. Though her heroes are always wonderfully handsome and incredibly rich, she still prefers her own loving husband.

Recent titles by the same author:

MANDATE FOR MARRAIGE

ON EQUAL TERMS

BY

CATHERINE O'CONNOR

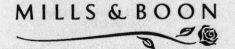

MILLS & BOON

MILLS & BOON, the Rose Device and LOVE ON CALL are trademarks of the publisher.
Harlequin Mills & Boon Limited,
Eton House, 18–24 Paradise Road, Richmond, Surrey TW9 1SR
This edition published by arrangement with
Harlequin Enterprises B.V.

© Catherine O'Connor 1995

ISBN 0 263 79080 0

Set in 10 on 12 pt Linotron Times
01-9508-52370

Typeset in Great Britain by CentraCet, Cambridge
Made and printed in Great Britain

CHAPTER ONE

KATE'S heart gave a sudden lurch. She watched in quiet desperation and disbelief as the formidable figure came striding towards her. She clutched the starched sheet in her tense fingers; the harsh cotton crackled but yielded little, despite the fierceness of her grip. Her knuckles turned white as her grip tightened still further, and her stomach twirled uncontrollably as Sebastian drew closer, coming to an abrupt stop in front of her.

'Kate,' he bit out, his tone clipped and curt, his sensuous mouth twisting into a bitter smile as he silently acknowledged the effect he was having on her. At the sound of his familiar voice Kate's eyes widened and her heart leapt into her dry throat as she stared at the sight of her stepbrother at the end of her hospital bed. She couldn't believe he had come for her and a spark of hope flickered inside her, warming the blood that now flowed quickly through her veins.

'Hello,' she managed in a breathless whisper, her head swimming and her heart beating out an increasingly rapid tattoo. She searched his face, her eyes aching with the effort as she sought some indication of affection, but his features were unreadable, a bronze, lifeless mask bereft of any expression.

'I've come to take you home.' His voice was freezing cold with icy indifference that made Kate's chest contract painfully. 'Now!' he snapped at her with

5

customary arrogance, and Kate had to prevent herself from nodding in agreement to his brusque order. The passing hope that he cared for her vanished as she recognised the familiar grim look.

'I'm not coming home,' Kate said firmly, trying to put a strength into her voice that she did not feel. She had only been in a minor road accident but she had been left bruised and badly shaken. The words were barely audible but he had heard them, and a sudden anger stiffened his jaw, a gleam illuminating his icy blue orbs with a spark of frosty light. His body was rigid as he kept an iron control.

'I'm not here to argue with you, Kate,' he told her, with a disapproving shake of his head. 'You're coming home, and that's final!' he said tersely, pulling open the bedside cabinet and throwing her clothes in a jumbled heap on the bed.

'You can't make me,' she protested indignantly. She was still recovering in hospital; surely he would not be allowed to take her home, especially against her will? Her eyes darted furiously around the open ward but there was no one in sight to help her. The patients were either asleep or in the day-room watching afternoon television.

'No?' he said softly, mocking her, as his eyes followed hers and scanned the desolate ward. He shrugged dismissively as his brows rose in derision.

'The doctors won't allow you to take me,' she pointed out, trying to be forceful, her voice cool—yet already she was beginning to panic. She knew just how ruthless her stepbrother could be! He had taken up partnership with her father, a partnership that by rights should have been hers. She certainly did not feel strong enough to stand up to him; her head was already beginning to ache as all the old bitterness swelled up inside her.

'On the contrary, my dear, they are more than delighted that I am taking responsibility for you,' he told her, the sense of victory ringing clearly in his tone. He fixed his icy blue eyes on her once more, a dangerous light flickering in their depths. 'Now dress,' he ordered curtly, pushing the pile of clothes closer to her. His expression was now crystal-clear and Kate read his disapproval: he did not like her new style. She made a protective grab for her clothes; they might have lacked the designer labels she had been used to, but at least she had afforded them without relying on anyone's help.

'Your taste in fashion certainly has changed,' Sebastian taunted.

'I no longer need a label to give me an identity.' Unlike some, she silently added, looking at his immaculate clothes quite deliberately.

'I never did,' he retorted briskly, putting Kate firmly in her place. 'I just prefer quality,' he continued.

'Don't we all, if we can afford it?' she replied tartly. She glared at him with heartfelt malice, her hands in a tight knot under the untidy pile of clothes as she clasped them together, trying to control the tremors.

'You have been given an allowance,' Sebastian growled angrily. 'A more than generous one,' he added with vehemence.

'I didn't want to use that,' she protested immediately. She suddenly felt defensive about her position, but couldn't understand why. She *wanted* to be independent. Besides, somehow it seemed wrong to use that money in the circumstances. She had left home after refusing to attend a select finishing school. It had caused a terrible family row and she knew whose fault that was—Sebastian's!

'No, you wouldn't want to use the money,' he snapped, breaking into her thoughts. 'My God, Kate, you really know how to hurt, don't you?' he snarled, his anger and bitterness spilling out.

Kate's head snapped back, her eyes molten pools of indignation. 'I wouldn't hurt anyone,' she denied, cut deeply by his accusation, and troubled by it. Why would he think *that* was her motivation—was his opinion of her so low?

'Never mind, I'll soon have you looking your usual self.' His sudden smile faded, as he picked up her thin blouse, holding the material between two of his slender fingers before dropping it back on to the bed.

'I don't want your charity!' Kate retorted, her voice strangely hoarse. 'I'm not even coming home,' she added forcefully. She couldn't face being with him and her emotions with regard to her father and stepmother were still in turmoil, though another bit of her wanted to be part of a family again.

'Believe me, Kate, you are—and now!' His lips widened to a dangerously sexy smile. Kate's stomach contracted painfully at his words; his suggestion sounded more like a threat, and she immediately felt herself grow hot at his remark. He assumed that she was willing to fall meekly back into her former life. She would not go with him! She threw back her head, her fair hair tumbling over her slim shoulders in disarray. She stared up at him, her heart racing, but she presented a calm façade, refusing to let him see the havoc he was creating within her.

'I've no intention of going home!' she spat at him, hating him with all her heart.

'And I've no intention of leaving here without you!' he bit back. He remained standing at the side of her bed, his hands placed firmly on his hips, pushing his tailored jacket back to reveal his hard chest, just visible beneath his white silk shirt. His expression was growing darker with every passing moment and the silence made Kate feel even more nervous. But she would not give in to him; it had taken her a long time to get over him and she wasn't prepared to risk the pain of rejection again.

'How did you know I was here?' Kate asked, trying to stall for time as she thought of a way to escape from him.

'A private detective. . .' he barked back, as if he was aware of her tactic and was finding it all rather tiresome. 'I had to find you,' he said. The words hung in the air between them. She heard the steely edge in his voice and knew she was to take that as a warning.

'Why?' she came back, unable to control herself in the face of such arrogance and the growing suspicion that he was not being totally honest with her.

'We can discuss that later; now let's go home,' he said with deceptive casualness. But his manner did not fool Kate. She knew him too well—knew that he was being evasive. Her determination to stand up to him wavered slightly as she recalled his formidable temper, but then the thought of going home failed her heart and mind, effectively blocking out her reservations about Sebastian. Yet what of her father—what was his view on all this? she wondered; it seemed strange that *he* had not come for her. Had he still not forgiven her, despite all her attempts to make amends?

'Where's my father?'

It was a simple enough question but she noticed the almost indefinable change that instantly came over Sebastian. She waited for him to speak. A cloud of darkness passed through his eyes but it was quickly gone.

'Does he know? Does he want me home?' she asked, her voice a mixture of hope and desperation. How she wanted his answer to be in the affirmative.

'Your sudden concern is heart-warming,' Sebastian drawled cruelly. 'Now get dressed, Kate.' His voice was heavy with contempt as he spun away from the bed and marched back down the ward. Kate stared after him. She was hurt by his tone. Her head was throbbing and she suddenly felt drained. It had not been the reunion she had wanted. She felt cheated, angry and humiliated. She looked down at the bundle of clothes he had thrown on the bed and knew she had neither the energy nor inclination to fight him. Once dressed, she made her way slowly up the ward. Something was wrong, she could tell, something that Sebastian was not telling her. But she knew that to ask him would be pointless. He would only tell her when he wanted to. He turned around as he heard her approach, his eyes raking over her and a frown furrowing his brow.

'You are all right, aren't you?' he asked, watching her closely. Kate matched his expression with a frown of her own. Was this genuine concern? she wondered.

It was the first time he had shown any interest in her well-being.

'I'll be all right.'

'Good,' was his monosyllabic reply, and Kate could discern nothing from it. He took her hand in his, his grip tight and possessive, as if he did not trust her not to try and escape. Her pulse immediately began to race; his touch still excited her, even after all this time.

Sebastian drove through the hectic traffic with his usual skill and speed and, within minutes, the city was being left behind. He exhaled noisily and shifted in his seat, and Kate saw him visibly begin to relax, yet she could still sense an underlying strain. The countryside was quiet; the roads, which in summer would be teeming with tourists, were completely empty. The green fields were varnished in a fine coating of frosty white rime and the trees stood stiffly erect, their slender branches like gnarled arms twisting upwards, reaching up into the sunless sky, stretching to find some heat. The only sign of activity was a host of black crows lining the greying fences of the roadside, waiting to pick at any unfortunate rabbit that might have been hit by a car. Kate gave an involuntary shiver; the day was as dark and dismal as the desolation she felt in her heart. The atmosphere in the car didn't help matters. It was strained; an invisible wall of resentment had been erected between them. The silence was so uncomfortable and fragile that she remained silent, gazing out of the window, her mind a flurry of emotions. Their last meeting had been far from harmonious and she wondered if he still remembered it. She did, so very clearly; she had secured herself a job and was leaving. She'd been determined to go but

Sebastian had stopped her in the hall, making one last attempt to persuade her to stay.

'Kate, stop it now,' he had said firmly, taking the case from her hand and placing it on the floor as he'd continued, 'It's not what you want—what any of us want.'

'What *I* want?' she exclaimed in outrage. She was still hurting from the fact that she had not been informed of the decision to send her away to a school until it had all been arranged. She should have been consulted—she wasn't a child; but that was how they treated her and she was determined to prove them all wrong. 'Who cares about what I want?' she threw at him, hating the fact that he had not jumped to her defence but had agreed with the idea. He wanted her to go, to be rid of her; his little stepsister was becoming a burden. And yet she still loved him.

'We all do, Kate.' Sebastian's voice was low, reasonable, but she didn't care. She was stung by his attitude, hurt more deeply than she was prepared to show.

'Really?' Her voice was thick with sarcasm, Sebastian's face distorted as he grabbed her by the arm.

'Yes,' he snapped, 'we *do* all care, and you're just being a damn fool.' A stubborn, sulky look covered her face and she raised her face to glare at him, shaking her arm loose from his grip.

'Listen, Kate,' he began again, trying a new tactic, still hoping to change her mind. 'Let's talk about it. If you're against the idea of going away to school, let's discuss some alternatives,' he suggested.

'I have an alternative,' she retorted swiftly. She had been forced to make her own arrangements, as he had taken over her rightful role in her father's business, but she wasn't prepared to tell him about her job—he would only mock. She enjoyed the startled look on his face, soon to be replaced by anger.

'It's ludicrous!' he snarled. 'How can you possibly hope to look after yourself? You're still a——'

'A child. . .' she cut in furiously at the insult. 'Wrong, Sebastian! That was an eighteenth birthday that we just celebrated—it makes me an adult,' she told him aloofly, trying to keep the pain from her voice. She tried so hard to make him see her as a grown-up, but it always failed. Now she was forcing the issue, but it seemed to make no difference.

'Then behave like one,' he responded coolly.

'I am!' Kate defended herself. 'I'm doing what I want.' She took hold of her suitcase, again determined to leave. Yet a crack of pain was beginning to break her heart.

'And no one matters,' he said brusquely, before adding in a softer tone, 'Not even me?'

Her eyes had flown to his at his words. She silently willed him to say more—to beg her not to leave, to tell her that he loved her—but he didn't, and she wanted to hurt him as he smashed her dreams.

'You least of all, Sebastian,' she ground out. 'If I ever see you again, it will be too soon.' Her face was distorted with pain and anger, her eyes fiery bright, and she turned away. Even as she opened the door she hoped he would say something—anything—even her name on his lips would have been enough—but he remained silent. She could feel the heat of his stare on her back but she refused to turn to say a final farewell.

A tear plumped at the corner of her eyes as she closed the door behind her. . . .

'I haven't had time for any lunch, so if you don't mind. . .' Sebastian began as he swung into the car park of a small country inn without waiting for a reply. His voice brought Kate sharply back to the present and she knew he remembered too what she had said to him all that time ago.

'No, not at all,' agreed Kate; she hadn't wanted to admit it but her nerves were on edge, because it was the first time she had been in a car since her accident. Though she had every confidence in Sebastian's driving, she was still glad of a little respite. It took her several moments to gain control of her unsteady limbs when she got out of the car and Sebastian offered no assistance—not that she would have accepted any, she thought angrily as she struggled to keep up with him. His long strides were eating up the distance in the car park.

'Sit near there,' he ordered, pointing her over to a snug corner next to a blazing log fire. 'You'll have something to eat.' It was an order, not a request, and Kate, too weary to argue, sank gratefully into the chair by the grate.

'I'll order coffee; it will help keep me awake,' he said as he removed his jacket and flung it carelessly over the back of a chair.

'That's fine,' smiled Kate, trying not to look at him, but already she knew she was fighting a losing battle. She was still totally aware of his masculinity. As she had noted in the hospital, the shirt he wore fitted to perfection around his muscular chest, drawing attention to a dark shadow of hair. He strode off to the bar with a smooth, confident air. Kate's eyes followed him, drawn hypnotically by the lithe movements of his body. She sighed; she had thought she was over him, that it was all in the past, but now she was no longer so sure. The heat of the fire warmed her chilled bones and she began to relax, despite the tense atmosphere.

'Are you enjoying your meal?' he asked later as he raised his glass to his mouth, his strong fingers encircling the stem. 'By the look of you, a decent meal is something you haven't had for some time.'

'I've been having a perfectly adequate diet,' she reported back through clenched teeth, almost hating how much she was enjoying the food; it made her feel slightly guilty. She knew she shouldn't, that it was pointless always to consider the problems of others, but she couldn't help it. She had been lucky finding a job through a local paper. She had worked for eighteen months, making her way up from office junior to the more senior post of co-ordinator. She worked for a Third World charity, and fighting hunger was now so important to her that it spilled out into her personal life, making her frugal. Sebastian shrugged, indifferent to her mood, neither annoyed nor amused by it.

'So you say,' he replied smoothly. His voice held a satisfied tone. 'But it hardly looks like it,' he added tauntingly.

Kate's temper was bubbling up inside her, like a volcano waiting to erupt. He knew exactly how to upset her. Even after all this time, he seemed to take a delight in annoying her! She kept looking firmly at him, refusing to allow him to dismiss her as if she were still a child. She confronted him squarely—she was an adult now. But he was unperturbed by her anger. He studied her carefully, then the citrus smell of his aromatic aftershave filled her nostrils as he moved closer to her.

'You look tired, Kate,' he said almost softly, and the sound of her name on his lips was touched with a sudden intimacy. 'I think we'd best hit the road again. I want you home as soon as possible.' She immediately detected the hidden message in his voice. There was something amiss, some problem he was not telling her.

'What is it, Sebastian? What's going on?' she demanded, her voice hoarse as sudden emotion gripped her.

'Not now, Kate, not here.' His voice held a finality that worried her even more.

'I want to know now,' she demanded again, troubled by his expression, her heart beating rapidly inside her, like a trapped bird.

'I'm tired, Kate, and so are you,' he told her firmly, brooking no argument.

'I want to know now!' Kate persisted, knowing that she sounded like a petulant child.

'I'm not prepared to discuss anything at the moment,' he told her, taking her arm, his fingers biting into her soft flesh. He escorted her out of the pub, his grip increasing as they went back to the car. Kate would have objected, but she suddenly didn't feel very well. She swayed slightly against him as the bitter wind seared through her fragile body.

'Kate—Kate, what is it?' He mumbled a curse as his arms wrapped around her swaying body, encircling her slender waist to steady her. Kate moaned slightly and pressed her fingers on her damp forehead. She had become over-excited and now she was paying for it.

'My head hurts,' she whispered softly. The pain-killers were wearing off and now her whole body ached. She felt exhausted, her eyes already closing as he pushed her gently into the car. He pulled her seatbelt across her, his hand accidentally brushing across her breast, and, for a second, he paused, his body stiffening. Then he closed the buckle with a snap.

'It's all right, I'll soon have you home, and then Dr Russell can check you over. There's nothing to worry about. The hospital said you were fine. You've just taken a bad knock,' he assured her briskly. He sounded confident, as usual, but Kate caught the flicker of doubt that flamed briefly in his eyes.

Kate closed her eyes and could remember nothing after that; it was all a hazy dream. Reality had become distorted through a veil of pain and shock.

'Sebastian,' she said, his name escaping through her dry, thinly parted lips in a hushed murmur. She desperately tried to focus on him, but her eyes ached and that dull pain throbbed incessantly in her head.

'Kate! Kate!' She heard the sound of his voice calling her name, far away in the distance, and she struggled to nod in response. She wanted to drift again, to fall back into the heavy sleep where she felt no pain. Here she felt like a trapped animal. She sensed that she was now in a room, and Sebastian was waiting and watching her every move. The events of the day slowly came back to her; she must have fainted. She certainly only had vague flitting pictures of what had gone before, yet she remembered immediately that something was wrong.

'Do you want a drink?' Sebastian's voice was soft, gentler than she remembered it, but the strength of his hands as they wrapped around her shoulders, raising her from the soft pillow, were the same. Strong, hard and muscular, lifting her with an ease that told her of his strength. The cold rim of a glass touched her dry lips and she drank thirstily of the water that was offered to her. She rested back on the pillow, forcing her lids open. The cold grey light of early morning filtered through the huge windows and Kate knew she was back, back in the house she had once called home. Sebastian was sitting on the bed. He looked tired. His eyes were red-rimmed through lack of sleep: the long drive had obviously taken its toll. His tobacco-coloured hair fell in disarray across his finely chiselled features. Kate felt a *frisson* race through her body, but she refused to let him see the effect he was having on her. He was still as handsome as ever, she thought bitterly, not liking the way she still responded to him.

'Welcome home,' he said, a ready smile forming on his sensuous mouth, as if he was unaware of the irony of his words. Kate nodded slowly, but did not return his smile.

Even Sebastian wouldn't ask that much, she thought wryly as she continued to study him. He hadn't really changed: there was only a touch of grey in his hair and there were no tell-tale signs of ageing around his clear blue eyes—and yet there was something. Kate felt it; that hidden thread that had always drawn them together alerted her to the fact that something about him had changed. But she was too tired to think about it now. Besides, it didn't concern her, not now. It was all in the past and best forgotten. She would have to leave here as soon as she had the chance; she would go back to her new life. However, already doubts had begun to surface at the back of her mind and she knew that it would be difficult, that Sebastian would be keeping a close eye on her, watching her every move.

'How are you?' he asked. 'The journey was too much and you passed out yesterday. That's why you've slept so long,' he continued, ignoring the fact that Kate had closed her eyes again. 'Are you still feeling drowsy?' he probed, his voice searing through her brain as she tried to shut him out. She hadn't been prepared for the impact that his return into her life would make, and she knew she had to keep him out of it in order to remain immune to him.

'Perhaps you'd like something to eat?' he offered. Kate's eyes flickered open; his voice seemed strangely formal and distant, but she didn't care. She closed her eyes again, determined to keep her fragile barriers firmly intact. She had to shut out his image, to secure her mind and heart against him. The reality that she was back with him was almost unbearable and every second in his presence would weaken her defences against him.

'I'd like a bath,' she managed; her speech sounded slurred. Kate knew a bath was her only chance of privacy and she wanted to be alone. She needed time alone, time to think, to rationalise her feelings, which swayed dramatically between hate and love for this man.

'A bath—yes, of course.' His tone was distinctly polite and Kate's eyes flickered open, searching the dark depths of his for a glimmer of tenderness, but there was none.

'It will probably bring you round a bit,' he informed her, patting her arm and sending an unexpected ripple of electric awareness through her body. He rose from the bed. Kate watched him cross the room. He moved with the same arrogant stride, liquid movements that belied his determination. She closed her eyes again, shutting out his image, but it was too late—already her mind had begun to drift back to their first meeting. . .

CHAPTER TWO

'GOOD morning.'

Kate gave a nervous start at the softly vibrant voice that cut through the early morning stillness. She spun round, fixing her eyes on the tall, broad-shouldered and immensely powerful-looking figure walking slowly towards her. A *frisson* of alarm ran through her body as her mind registered the sheer power of the man. He towered over her own petite stature and looked down at her. His eyes were dark blue, with thick, curly lashes, and his hair was a mixture of browns, sort of tobacco-coloured.

'My name's Sebastian,' he said, his voice deep and clear, as he extended his hand in a formal greeting. Kate gazed up at him, her eyelids blinking anxiously as she noted the teasing lilt in his tone.

'Hello, Sebastian,' she managed, at the man who was now her stepbrother and her senior by twelve years.

'I'd thought I'd take Dylan out,' Sebastian said smoothly, releasing her hand and moving into the stalls. Kate nearly sagged with relief at his words.

'He's all ready, Mr. . .' she began, but Sebastian swung round, his blue eyes dark.

'Sebastian—please. My name is Sebastian.'

'Sebastian,' agreed Kate, with a nod. It seemed odd to her that he should want to be called by his first name. The timbre in his voice held the unmistakable tone of authority and Kate knew he expected to be obeyed. 'Dylan is ready and eager to be out,' Kate said, instinct warning her that Sebastian was not as malleable as her father. He was wearing riding boots but the rest of his clothes were far from formal. He wore a pair of faded denim jeans that hugged his muscular thighs and a checked shirt peeked out around the crew neck of a thick navy sweater. He could have passed for an Englishman. But Kate had eavesdropped on many adult conversations, so knew his heritage, even if his mother was at pains to forget all about her disastrous first marriage. She had been married to a much older man, a fiery Italian who believed a woman's place was in the home. Sebastian had inherited his father's dark looks, his fiery disposition, but his ideas on women were far removed from his father's. Still, Kate would have known immediately that he wasn't English. There was something wild about him—untamed and free—unlike the wealthy English gentlemen that she was familiar with. His hair was streaked with flecks of shimmering gold and it was swept back off his face like a sleek lion's mane, drawing attention to his autocratic features. His eyes were blue, yet they were dark with a piercing quality, like an icy shaft of light. Kate sensed even then that she would always love him, that somehow they were kindred souls who had been drawn together by circumstances beyond their control. She stared up at him, her pale grey eyes almost hidden beneath her long, straight fringe of ash-blonde hair.

'Dylan is a fine horse, such a beautiful grey stallion,' she breathed, following Sebastian into the stalls, wanting to be close to him.

'He needs far too much exercise,' Sebastian commented as he began to lead the horse out.

Kate was still following, like a young puppy eager to please its new master.

'Do you ride?' Sebastian asked, suddenly turning his attention to Kate, and he managed to control the smile of amusement that tugged at his lips when she coloured again instantly. Kate nodded silently in childish awe of the man. 'Then saddle up; we can both go for a ride.'

'Your bath is ready.'

The sound of Sebastian's voice shattered her dream and Kate opened her eyes and nodded.

'Thanks,' she said, quickly lowering her long lashes over her eyes before he had time to read the depths of emotion in them.

'Let me help you,' Sebastian offered, moving towards the bed; but he stopped instantly as he saw Kate stiffen.

'I'm quite capable of finding my own way to the bathroom.'

'I'm sure you are.' His mouth tightened. As he'd spoken a flame of anger had briefly flared in the normally ice-cool depths of his eyes. Kate glared back at him. It was always the same between them—a constant round of battles, and she was growing weary of them.

'I can manage,' she said. She wanted to be strong, to show him she could now do without him. She had changed in the last two years, had become self-sufficient. Had it not been for the unfortunate car accident, he would have never found her. She had a new life, and she had learned to cope, to accept the fact that she was no longer welcome in her childhood home. It had been hard but she had managed—without Sebastian's help, without anyone's help. Kate swallowed, trying to rid herself of any bitterness. It would do no one any good. Besides, she was home now; perhaps her father would finally accept her back into the fold. She sat up, pushing the crisp, warm sheets from her body. Her eyes dropped to her legs. How thin they looked. Had she lost that much weight? she mused momentarily, before urging her body upwards. She swayed slightly as she got up, the after-effects of the accident making her unsteady. Sebastian reacted quickly, instantly at her side, his arm offering an unwelcome support. Kate pulled away. It was all his fault. She was here, back at home, with no sign of her father. Sebastian had been wrong to bring her home; she had not been forgiven.

'Leave me alone,' she ground out at him through clenched teeth. The knowledge that her father hadn't come to see her hurt her more than she cared to admit. Sebastian's face darkened at her words, but he remained silent, viewing her with such cold contempt that Kate felt chilled to the bone, the heat of her temper evaporating under his steely gaze.

'I don't want or need your help,' she scoffed.

'Don't you?' Sebastian questioned, with an amused raise of his eyebrows as Kate's body swayed slightly again.

'No,' Kate snapped back, but too soon; her legs suddenly gave way and, had it not been for Sebastian's quick actions, she certainly would have fallen to the floor.

'Kate!' he admonished, his voice gruff and strangely at odds with the concern that flickered in his face. He swept her hair from her face, the rough hairs on the back of his hand rubbing against the smooth, soft skin of her cheeks. Kate felt an immediate rush of heat. His touch still held the same potent magic for her and the realisation made her feel dangerously vulnerable.

'I'm all right,' she said. She made her voice sound strong, hoping that it sounded like a statement when in fact it was a plea for survival. She was already weakening. Her female instincts seemed determined to betray her. She pushed her hand against his hard chest. It was a futile gesture, like hitting a brick wall. Her hand made no impact on his muscular frame. She stood up, moving away from him, aware of his growing impatience.

She willed her weak legs to support her as she made her way tentatively to the bathroom. She slammed the door behind her, shutting Sebastian out, then she leant back on it, desperate for the solid support it could offer her. Her shoulders sagged with the weight of despair and her knees buckled with fatigue. She didn't want Sebastian's pity, his brotherly concern, yet it was all he was willing to offer her. The realisation that she was still vulnerable to him made her angry.

She slipped out of her over-sized nightshirt and stepped cautiously into the bath. It was wonderful; the hot water, made silky-soft with delicately scented oils, lapped against her aching body, slowly massaging away her physical pains. But her lonely heart still ached. Nothing had really changed. She breathed deeply,

inhaling the heavenly fragrance. The sweet smell of
summer flowers made her mind drift back to happier
times, as if drawn by a hidden power source that she
was too weak to fight.

CHAPTER THREE

SHE was a young girl again, lying in the meadow, the summer grass high; the wild flowers were in glorious abundance, shooting up between the verdant green. The sun was a brilliant yellow disc of heat, burning on to her bare legs as she lay day-dreaming, heedless of everything except the fact that Sebastian was coming home. It had been months since she had seen him and the separation had been almost unbearable. He had been in America, working on Wall Street, but he had now returned to England, still working in commodities on the Stock Exchange. He came home only at weekends, keeping a penthouse flat in London for the week. Kate longed for those weekends, hating Sunday evenings, when he drove away, leaving her for another week.

She hadn't heard him approach and at first she took no notice of the tickling grass that played across her cheeks; she felt lazy; it was too hot to move. Finally, as her hand attempted for the tenth time to brush the offending grass away, she reluctantly opened her eyes. It was like a dream, as if she had thought about him so much that he had suddenly materialised before her! He was leaning over her, his face tantalisingly close, and she lifted herself up closer to him, instinctively placing her soft, warm lips on his, kissing him with sweet innocence.

'Kate!' He laughed. She could still hear it now,

echoing through her mind, teasing, mocking, cutting into her heart. He had not been offended or perturbed—or even aroused, she added to herself ruefully. To him, she was still a child. He had been blissfully unaware of the changes her body had been going through, while she had watched her growing development with daily interest, hoping with each swell of her tender young breasts that Sebastian would finally see her as a woman. . .

Kate slipped deeper into the soapy water till the water splashed up against her cheeks. How hard she had tried to become the woman Sebastian wanted, copying the looks and styles of the women-friends he had. That innocent kiss had been the first of many attempts to capture his attention, but it had all been in vain; all Kate had managed to arouse was her stepmother's wrath and her father's disapproval. She could still hear Clare's voice ringing in her ears.

'Really, Kate, you should leave Sebastian alone. Find friends of your own age,' her stepmother had complained on numerous occasions, but Kate had ignored her, always ignored her.

'I don't want friends my own age,' she had retorted frostily, hating Clare for interfering.

'Clare's right, Kate. Why not invite some of your own friends home?' Her father had supported his new wife, which had hurt Kate deeply.

'Clare is right, Clare is right,' she'd mimicked back. 'Isn't she always?' she'd added bitterly. 'As for bringing friends home, I haven't a home any more—not since she came.'

Clare had flinched at her words but remained silent.

'Really, Kate!' admonished her father. 'There's no need to be rude.'

'I'm going out,' Kate had snapped back, heedless of his opinion and slamming the door as she left. It had been a scene played out many times, till Kate had felt trapped in the role and unable to escape.

The thought of her parents made Kate begin to scrub at her body with the coarse loofah, as if in an attempt to rub out the past. She knew that was impossible; all her attempts to make amends had been disregarded. She was back home now—soon, perhaps, she would see her father again. The thought of being reconciled made her heart leap with sudden joy.

She stayed in the bath till the water chilled. She wanted to be alone to try and sort out her feelings. Eventually, however, she got out, wrapping a warmed fluffy towel about her body. Wiping the condensation from the mirror, she stared blankly at her reflection. She pushed damp tendrils of hair from her face and moved closer, peering at the dull image of her face. She was pale, her eyes lifeless, with dark rings brought on by a poor diet and lack of sleep. They were swollen and bruised as a result of the accident. Tentatively she raised her hand, touching her face gently, moving her fingers lightly over her eyes, and flinching at the pain that even the gentlest of touches caused. She rubbed at her forehead wearily. Her head still ached and she couldn't remember quite what had happened—it all seemed so unreal, like a bad dream.

'Kate! Are you OK? Kate! Kate!' Sebastian's voice was growing louder. It was accompanied by the rattling of the door-handle and his fist hammering against the solid wood panels till the door shook. Kate gripped the luxuriously soft peach towel about her body as a defensive wall. She turned the key, opening the door with deliberate slowness.

'Are you all right?' Sebastian demanded sharply, stepping closer, his arms catching her slender shoulders in a firm grip. Kate's skin burned as his fingers touched her soft flesh. She caught the scent of his familiar aftershave.

'Yes, I'm fine,' she snapped, shrugging herself free as she moved, hating the effect he was having on her. She tensed herself for his touch as she went through the doorway, passing close to him but avoiding his outstretched hands. He dropped his arms in a sudden gesture of defeat. A frustrated frown creased his forehead.

'There's no need to snap. You've only yourself to blame,' he reminded her grimly, following her back into the bedroom, his eyes burning into her back. Kate spun round. All the pent-up feelings she felt for him spilled out in a torrent.

'Me?' she practically screamed. '*I'm* to blame?' She echoed his words in furious disbelief. 'How do you make that out? It was a car accident.'

'An accident you would not have been involved in had you been at home,' Sebastian reminded her in a chilling tone. Kate shook her head at his words. She felt she could stand up to him now. She was no longer a child, though the familiar sense of being unloved surfaced at his words.

'This was my home before you and your mother arrived,' she told him as all the old pain and bad memories swelled up inside her. It had been traumatic enough, her father's suddenly remarrying. Kate had felt so rejected. The small amount of time her father had had for her when not working now had to be shared with his new wife and her son. It had been so hard; how she had hated them both. Yet, despite everything, now Kate realised just how homesick she had been, how much she had really missed them all. The effects of the accident had only increased her stress.

'Stop it, Kate; stop feeling sorry for yourself, and stop blaming others for your own silly mistakes,' Sebastian growled, his voice dangerously low in comparison to her heartfelt scream.

'It's true! It's all your fault, you and your mother's,' she threw back, heedless of the way his whole frame suddenly stiffened.

'What about your father, Kate? Isn't he to blame as well?' Sebastian replied in a low voice. 'He did marry my mother,' he concluded, a smile tugging at his mouth.

'My father always loved me,' she protested, as she thought of the terrible argument she had had with him the last time they had spoken.

It came racing up, forcing itself from the dark, deep recesses of her mind. She could see it so clearly, the four of them, as if locked into a time-warp. Her father was in front of the blazing fire, Clare, her stepmother, was sitting on the edge of a chair, obviously a little nervous, and Sebastian was there with the smear of tell-tale red lipstick still on his face. Kate stood alone, staring in disbelief at her father's words. It couldn't be true.

'You're offering Sebastian *my* partnership?' she

cried in horror, her eyes flying to Sebastian, suddenly hating him with all her might.

'No, Kate,' her father said, softly but firmly. 'It's just that I have other plans for you at the moment. . .'

'Other plans? What other plans? I want to join you in the family business,' she protested furiously. She had worked so hard to understand the work involved—now it was all for nothing.

'Clare has found a suitable school for you in France.' Her father paused as he saw the look of dismay sweep over his daughter's face. 'It's just for a couple of years. It will broaden your horizons.'

'I don't want my horizons broadened—and nor does she.' Kate glared at her stepmother with unconcealed contempt. 'She just wants me out of the way so her son can take over the business.'

'That's not true, Kate. . .' Clare began, but Kate turned her back on her, refusing to listen. How she regretted that action later. Her father reacted instinctively, pulling at Kate, anger and hurt vying for supremacy.

'Apologise, Kate, at once,' he demanded, but Kate remained resolute, her lip protruding stubbornly.

'No, no, I won't! It's the truth, only you're too blind to see it! And he,' she said, swinging her hand out to point accusingly at Sebastian, 'he's not family. What does he care about our traditions? He's just a money-maker!'

'Kate! Kate!' her father cried again. 'Apologise at once!' But Kate was too filled with emotion. How could he do this to her, take their sides against her? It was all so wrong.

'I won't, and I won't stay where I'm not wanted.

You have a son now, so you don't need me,' Kate cried as her heart broke in two and she fled the room.

Two days later she had left. All attempts she had made to get in touch with her family since then had been rejected, leaving her desolate. She had never received even one reply.

'Why the past tense?' Sebastian asked her now, as if unaware of the strained relationship between her father and herself. 'He still loves you, but you're not a child any more, Kate, you have to understand that he loves my mother as well,' he explained gently, as if he *were* speaking to a child. Kate seethed inwardly. *She* was an adult—she understood! But would Sebastian always insist on seeing her as if she had never grown up? Did he really think that her reason for not returning home was because of her stepmother? Surely he knew that her father had ignored all her attempts at a reconciliation? 'I understand that.' She almost laughed. 'I accepted their marriage a long time ago.'

'Did you, Kate?' Sebastian questioned her grimly, and her eyes flew to his. Surely he must realise why she couldn't return home? Surely he hadn't forgotten what had passed between them, and the terrible consequences? His eyes rested on hers, blank and unreadable.

'Of course I've accepted their marriage, for God's sake. They've been married eight years!' she bit back at him, hurt by his lack of understanding. She knew she had been difficult when her father had first remarried, but she had been a child and not used to sharing her father's affection with anyone. The adjustment to sharing his love had not been easy but she had grown to accept his new relationship, hard though it had been. She had carefully hidden her pain behind a mask of outrage.

'Then why did you run away?' Sebastian challenged. 'When you should have come home?' he added.

'I couldn't,' she protested angrily, not wanting to explain, to let him know he had won everything—the business and her father.

'You mean wouldn't!' he returned.

'You don't understand—surely——' Kate began, but Sebastian interrupted, anger sharpening his voice to a rapier edge, cutting deeply into her heart.

'Oh, grow up! You just ran away,' he snapped.

'I didn't run away,' she protested indignantly. She was ashamed to admit the truth that her father had not wanted her here. She didn't want to give him the satisfaction of knowing the awful truth. . . 'I chose to live away from home, and I'm twenty this year— hardly a child,' she informed him crisply, ignoring the mocking rise of his dark eyebrows. 'I've grown up a lot in the last couple of years——' she began to explain, suddenly wanting him to know the work she had been doing. She was so proud of it. She had to make him realise the past was behind them.

'Physically perhaps,' Sebastian cut in, his eyes making a swift inventory of her slender body. But Kate ignored his appraisal; she was still too angry with him. He was putting her down, refusing to acknowledge that she was no longer a child, totally disregarding what she was saying, and she was incensed.

'I'm not a child any more, Sebastian,' she managed to say calmly, despite her annoyance and the fact that her stomach felt weak under his cold scrutiny.

'You certainly behave like one,' he said sharply.

'I don't!' Kate came back, hating the way her impulsive denial sounded so immature. Sebastian's expression showed his dry amusement at her remark. Kate seethed. He would never know how she had longed to return home, but there had been a myriad other reasons, too, why she couldn't, reasons that he still seemed oblivious to. What about the relationship that had been developing between them? It hurt that he didn't seem to have thought of that at all. It was true that she had not been welcome here, but she had also wanted some independence. A chance to show her parents that she had changed, become responsible, that she was no longer the spoilt, selfish child. The work she did now made her realise just how privileged she had been, which made her feel uncomfortably guilty sometimes.

'Then you don't consider running off and upsetting your father childish behaviour? I've wasted quite a lot of money over the last few months searching for you,' Sebastian growled. His face was dark with intent, lightened only by the fierce light that flamed in his blue eyes. Kate felt her anger bubble up again inside her. It seemed to feed off him. He just wasn't prepared to listen. He wouldn't even give her the chance to explain.

'I'm sorry you wasted your money. You should have left me where I was and your money in the bank,' she replied.

'Left you in that tawdry flat, with that man? How long do you think you would have survived?' Sebastian asked.

'I happen to like that flat. OK, it was a little run-down, but it was cheap,' she defended herself. Terry, her boss, shared all the expenses, making it very economical.

'I can believe that.' A smile touched the corners of Sebastian's mouth as he enjoyed her flaring temper. Kate knew what he was implying and she was furious. Did he not realise that she worked? That Terry and she were merely flatmates? She would not lower herself to explain. It might do him good to think she had a relationship with Terry. She tossed her head back as she spun away from him and marched over to her dressing-table, throwing herself down heavily on the chair. It creaked in protest. She glared at his reflection in the mirror.

'I'd rather be on my own,' she told him aloofly as she picked up a hairbrush and made a desultory attempt at brushing her damp hair. She hoped that her cold attitude was coolly dismissive but Sebastian remained impassive.

'Quite the Greta Garbo, aren't we?' he mocked, his generous mouth widening still further while her mouth thinned to a grim line. He folded his arms across his muscular chest, his stance warning her that he had no intention of leaving. She knew how stubborn Sebastian could be.

'Shut up, Sebastian. Shut up and get out,' Kate shouted, unable to stand his presence any longer. His taunting smile only reflected his lack of understanding. He raked his fingers through his hair and shook his head, tutting softly at her outburst.

'Now that's not very polite, is it?' he teased. 'I see your manners haven't improved. Clare was right—you should have gone to a finishing school.'

But Kate was in no mood to be taunted. She was determined to wipe the smile from his arrogant face.

'Clare still managed to get rid of me,' she turned to remind him. She hoped the jibe would hit home. But her sense of victory was quickly squashed. For a moment there was a flicker of annoyance on his face but then he grinned, his eyes bright with humour.

'Of course! It was the wicked stepmother,' he said dramatically, laughing as he raised his hand to his forehead, as if he were part of a Victorian melodrama.

'Well, it was, wasn't it?' she said coolly, trying to ignore his mocking attitude and the obvious amusement she was affording him.

'Yes, my mother did suggest you should go away for a while. It was a sensible decision in the circumstances,' he said, his voice taking on another edge. His tone warned her that he had totally agreed with that decision. So, he was as much to blame as Clare, perhaps even more so. Kate tried to suffocate the flush of discomfort she was feeling. She rallied, suddenly wanting to turn the tables on him.

'And what circumstances were they?' she asked, her eyes bright with a challenging gleam.

Sebastian sighed loudly and shook his head. He viewed her like an adult looking at a disobedient child. He sunk his hands deep into his trousers pockets, till the material of his trousers was stretched across his flat stomach.

'Why, Kate, do you insist on making life difficult?' he growled, his jaw tensing with annoyance. 'Aren't there enough problems in the world without you adding to them?' he continued. His tone was weary, as if she were still a besotted schoolgirl in total awe of him.

'Problems? Doesn't that just sum it up? In your eyes I was a problem, so you all decided to ship me off to school,' Kate retorted, flicking her hair back from her shoulders as she stood up to face him. 'But naughty Kate wouldn't do as she was told,' she taunted. How, in reality, she had hated going away, leaving him and her family and friends. The same sense of hurt and betrayal still gnawed away at her, despite the fact that it had been almost two years ago. He had remained here, at home, while she had become the outcast, struggling to prove to him that she was an equal.

'It wasn't like that, Kate, and you know it,' Sebastian reminded her, his voice dangerously quiet and his features softening.

'Wasn't it?' she returned, wrinkling her nose in an expression of scorn as she moved closer to him, her body aching for a response, even if all she got was an arousal of his wrath.

'No,' he cut in sharply. 'You were getting out of hand—surely you remember?' His eyes searched her face for some trace of understanding.

'I remember all right, Sebastian,' she answered. She remembered the pathetic lengths she had gone to in order to secure his attention in the past. That fateful evening had made her realise how foolish she had been, and it was branded on her mind, her heart and her soul forever. 'I remember it very well.' She moved closer, still hoping she could make him weaken, but not understanding why. 'A kiss in the dark, that's all. Wasn't it, Sebastian?' she goaded, watching the streak of colour that highlighted his cheeks as his gaze fell on her heaving breasts as they rose from the cover of the towel.

'For goodness' sake, Kate, grow up!' he barked, his dark eyes turning to pools of black ink.

'Wasn't that the problem—that I did grow up?' she taunted, her head tilted back, her eyes ablaze with defiance. Now his face was white with anger, his jaw tight and hard like granite. His eyes trapped hers with a piercing light that almost seared into the depths of her soul. Kate was frozen to the spot, her heart beating furiously. But she refused to drop her gaze. She stared up at him defiantly. She had grown up a great deal in the past eighteen months, working in a busy office, often forced to take on extra responsibilities, and now this was her chance to prove it. Sebastian remained silent, and for a fleeting moment Kate thought she caught a flicker of interest in his expression, but it disappeared so quickly that she decided she had imagined it. The stillness only heightened the increasingly tense atmosphere and she waited silently, trying to force a response from him. Suddenly he turned on his heel and marched away, the slamming of the door confirming that he had gone. Kate sank in disbelief on to her bed. What on earth had possessed her to act in that way? She threw herself back on to the soft pillows in frustration. Why did she always have to react to him? Her own words came back into her mind to taunt her: 'A kiss in the dark.'

How well she remembered it! It had been her eighteenth birthday—the house had been filled with family and friends for the celebration. Kate had known Sebastian would come, even though she had seen little of him over the last few months. She'd known he would be there that night. Her heart had flipped every time she'd heard the doorbell ring then sank again when it wasn't him. Finally he had arrived. She could see it now, like watching a film on the screen. She had raced to the door, flinging herself into his arms.

'Sebastian, I knew you'd come,' she cried. Her arms clung around his neck and she rejoiced in the intoxicating aroma of him that enveloped her whole body.

'Kate.' His tone was abrupt, almost curt, and he pushed her firmly away from him. It was as if she had been slapped, the pain was so real. She stepped away, bewildered; she was eighteen now, a young woman. She had made so much effort tonight, dressing with so much care, in a dress which she knew perhaps was a little too sophisticated for her but she had seen his other girlfriends wear such designs. He had disentangled himself from her as if embarrassed, and Kate felt her blood turn to ice as he introduced her to his stunning companion, who had just stepped into the house.

'Kate, this is Louisa.' His arm wrapped around the woman's slender waist and he drew her up against him.

Kate gave a bitter smile at the memory. How shocked she had been—totally stunned. She had truly believed it was only a matter of time before Sebastian would confess his love for her. Unbidden tears now pricked her eyes and she rolled over on the bed, unable to stop their salty flow at the memory of that fateful night. She had gone outside in the garden until finally Sebastian had come in search of her. She had been cold, but her body had been shivering more with anticipation than the night air.

'Kate, you'll catch your death in that flimsy thing,' he had laughed, pulling her gently against his warm chest, and Kate had allowed her head to fall against him, listening to the steady thud of his strong heart, breathing in the very essence of him.

'Do you like my dress?' she whispered, raising her doe eyes to look at him. He looked at her, smiling, and nodded.

'Quite the young lady,' he said, but she had known he was sincere and her heart had leapt at his words. She moved closer, and lifted her face to his, her full lips parted in soft invitation, her eyes holding a slumberous warmth.

'Kate,' he whispered, so quietly, as if it was an incantation of love. 'My Kate.' He allowed his hand to travel over her tender cheek and she inclined her head like a satisfied cat, to enjoy the feel of it on her skin. She knew he was going to kiss her; she had imagined it so many times that it seemed perfectly natural. She stepped closer and their bodies fused together in silent communion. He lowered his head and Kate closed her eyes, savouring every moment. His lips met hers in gentle surrender and Kate felt herself soaring, soaring higher and higher.

'Sebastian!' The shocked, disapproving tone of Louisa broke the spell, banishing the magic moment. Kate heard Sebastian mumble apologies and the realisation that to him it had all been a mistake chilled her to the bone. He moved away from her, leaving her feeling lost and alone in an alien world. She knew then that he didn't love her, not the way she loved him.

The rest of her birthday party had been a fiasco. Sebastian spent the whole evening with Louisa, dancing closely, sharing jokes, snatching kisses like typical young lovers. Kate watched them, her insides twisting painfully at every sign of intimacy between them. She hadn't wanted to go away but knew now that there was little to keep her at her family house.

Kate sighed and pushed herself upright. It was all in the past, she reminded herself firmly. It had been a silly schoolgirl crush, an infatuation with an older man. She was past all that now—she no longer loved Sebastian. She hated him, in fact, hated his arrogance, his superior attitude. All she wanted now was the chance to prove to him just how little he meant to her.

CHAPTER FOUR

KATE began to dress, pulling open familiar drawers and taking out some delicate underwear, and suddenly rejoicing in the luxury she had been denying herself. She gave a start as she heard the door open and swung round to face Sebastian as he viewed her in her skimpy underwear.

'Why so startled, Kate?' he enquired. Kate grabbed at her dressing-gown, drawing the cord firmly around her body, but she still felt bare, exposed, under his cold scrutiny.

'It's polite to knock before entering a lady's bedroom,' she retorted. She had immediately gone on the attack as it was her only protection against him. She still felt oddly vulnerable with him, despite the fact that all she felt for him was loathing.

'I've brought you breakfast in bed,' Sebastian replied, with a calm smile. He seemed to ignore the look on Kate's face. Here we go again, Kate thought to herself. He's treating me as if I'm the baby sister needing to be looked after. But she had to concede that despite his usual customary arrogance he sounded sincere.

'Breakfast in bed?' she echoed. 'That's hardly necessary.' She laughed, touched by his sudden gesture of kindness yet troubled by it, too.

'It is, because that's where you're to stay for a least two days,' Sebastian said firmly as he placed the tray on the side-table and inclined his head towards the bed, expecting her to get back into it immediately.

'Two days!' repeated Kate miserably. She would go mad! She hated being inactive—and Sebastian knew that.

'That's right; now get back in.' Sebastian gave an indulgent twitch of his mouth, as if he expected her to protest. Kate grimaced to herself at his arrogant assumption that she would do as he said.

'I feel fine,' she protested, moving away from the bed and over to the tray of food; the delicate aroma of smoked bacon had awakened a sudden feeling of hunger in her. Sebastian shrugged his broad shoulders, obviously indifferent to her claims.

'That's debatable. However, they're doctor's orders—not some devious idea thought up by me,' he informed her. He knew she held him responsible.

Kate turned away, lowering her sooty long lashes over her eyes. 'I think he's over-reacting, then,' she said stubbornly. The thought of being trapped in bed still filled her with dread. She had been so busy, used to working all hours, and even then all her energy had not been spent.

'It was a very nasty accident; it could have been fatal,' Sebastian reminded her.

Kate shivered as a sudden image of the out-of-control car spinning towards her flashed through her mind. She gripped the edge of the table for support, suddenly feeling sick.

'That's why bed-rest has been recommended,' he continued, a tiny note of triumph in his voice. His arms were round her shoulders as he guided her back to the bed. Kate's muscles set against his touch but she felt too weak to protest as he helped her. She lay down on the bed, grateful now for Sebastian's support. She looked up at him, smiling her thanks weakly, but he withdrew his hands quickly and looked away.

'You'll feel better after you've eaten.' There was a strange tension in his voice.

Kate's eyes flickered down to the tray of food. There seemed to be a huge amount—more like a full brunch than a light breakfast! She looked back at Sebastian, searching for some trace of—what? She knew that all she would find was his contempt. He felt no sympathy for her, only duty. She tried to read what lay behind the cool, intelligent mask—what type of game he was playing with her.

'There's far too much here. . .' she began.

'Kate, this is one point I refuse to argue about.' Sebastian's gaze narrowed on her militant expression. 'I am not going to repeat this at every meal. I don't know what the hell you've been doing with yourself but you look a mess. You've lost weight, and before you see your father you'll have to look a damn sight better.' He paused for a second to place a silencing finger on Kate's lips as her mouth opened, ready to protest again. He continued, his eyes warning her to be silent, 'So each and every meal which is served I expect you to eat—all of it. Understood?' he pronounced sternly.

Kate's protests died on her lips when she saw the uncompromising look that was carved on Sebastian's face. She knew that, as far as he was concerned, there was going to be no more discussion on this matter; he was determined.

'The longest Daddy's ever away is a few days. I can

hardly eat that much in such a short space of time that it could make any difference. . .' she tried once more, her argument going off on a tangent, but Sebastian cut in forcefully.

'He's not here. Our parents are in Kenya. . .'

'At this time of year?' she asked after a while, slightly puzzled. She took a mouthful of hot coffee and was about to launch into a million questions, but the bed sank with the weight of Sebastian's body as he sat down. There was something in his expression, a seriousness that shone in his eyes, that caused a sudden whirl of panic to surge through Kate.

'What is it?' she demanded as she struggled to keep the strain from her voice.

He took a slow, deep breath, while Kate waited.

'Your father has been ill. They've gone to the villa for an extended holiday to help in his recuperation.' His voice was clinical. He could have been reading the news, not informing her that her father was seriously ill. It was well-known that Howard Peterson was a workaholic, who never took holidays unless forced to and even then work was never that far away. Kate tried to comprehend what Sebastian had just told her. It couldn't possibly be true. Her father was a strong, vital man; he had never been ill in his life.

'Why are you saying this?' she accused Sebastian, wanting so much for it to be a cruel trick on his part. Her eyes searched his face, hoping and waiting for his denial, but none came.

'I'm sorry, Kate, there was no easy way of telling you. I know it's a shock. . .' His voice now held little comfort.

'What happened? What's wrong with him?' She

didn't care now about appearances; she was not going to hide her emotions. She couldn't; they were far too strong. Her hand reached out, grasping Sebastian's arm tightly. 'What happened?' she demanded again. 'Tell me what's wrong. You should have told me sooner, at once. . .'

'I've told you now because I feel you're strong enough. I wasn't sure before that you were ready for the news,' Sebastian said quietly.

'You had no right to keep this information from me. He's my father,' Kate shouted with sudden possessiveness. Sebastian shrugged his arm free of her grip with a sudden jerk, and Kate's hand dropped limply on to the bed. His eyes raked over her with derision.

'So the prodigal daughter is now concerned?' he mocked her. 'A little too late to play the dutiful child, aren't we?' he scoffed. Kate flinched at his tone. She sat stunned, in silence.

'Tell me what's wrong with my father,' she persisted, ignoring Sebastian's contempt.

'Why the sudden interest, Kate? Feeling guilty?' Sebastian almost sneered. Kate felt suddenly leaden; surely he was not blaming her for her father's ill-health?

'For God's sake, Sebastian, tell me,' she urged, her voice hoarse with emotion.

'He had a heart attack,' Sebastian said simply, but Kate heard the crack in his voice and knew then that he too was concerned.

She sat, struggling to accept the idea. Finally, she whispered, 'When?'

Sebastian looked directly at her as he heard the unspent emotion in her voice.

'Three months ago. . .'

'Three months? I should have——' Kate began, but Sebastian was in no mood to give any quarter.

'Yes, you should have been here, and had you been he might have recovered. As it is. . .' His voice trailed away, leaving Kate in turmoil.

'What is it?'

'He's not making the recovery he should. Progress has been slow, hence the holiday,' he told her coolly.

'Thank God you came when I had that accident, otherwise I might never have found out,' Kate breathed, with some measure of relief.

'You don't honestly believe I came to the hospital out of concern for *you*?' Sebastian said evenly. 'I saw the effect your absence was having on him. Despite your appalling behaviour, he actually still loves you.'

Kate listened, horrified. She had wanted so much to make amends to her father but he had refused to accept her offers of reconciliation. Surely Sebastian knew that any ill-feeling was all on her father's side?

'You don't understand. . .' she protested, hurt and anger vying for supremacy as she caught the flash of scorn in his eyes.

'Don't I?' he said heavily, pushing himself from the bed. 'I understand very well, Kate. You're nothing but a spoilt, self-centred child who cares for no one else but yourself.' He strode over to the window and gazed out across the hills, not bothering even to look at her.

Kate recoiled, stung by his words. He was wrong—terribly, terribly wrong—but she couldn't tell him the truth. It would be a betrayal of her father and she loved him too much for that. Instead she would have to allow Sebastian to think badly of her. Besides, she wouldn't be staying here now—she had to go out to see her father at once.

'I'll go today,' Kate said, pushing the half-eaten tray of food from her lap and scrambling out of bed. Perhaps she was too late? She shook her head to dismiss the thought from her brain; it was too awful even to contemplate. She flung open her wardrobe doors and stared at the barren space; a handful of wire coat-hangers hung empty, confirming her worst fears. She spun round to face Sebastian.

'Where are my clothes?' she demanded, her teeth clenched together so tightly that her jaw ached with the effort.

'Clothes!' he said with unhidden contempt. 'Those rags that you have started wearing? I didn't even bother to pick them up. I left them all behind.'

His arrogance made her blood boil.

'You've done what?' Kate said, her voice shrill with incredulity. She knew her anger was amusing him; had he not always taken delight in teasing her? She refused to allow him to see her weakness. 'You had no right. . .' she began, the words coming out in a strange whisper.

'I had every right. In time you will be well enough to go to see your father. For that you will require a wardrobe of suitable clothes—none that you owned fell into that category,' Sebastian reminded her with his usual ease.

'I want to go now!' Kate tried to inject some strength into her voice but failed. She knew she had sounded more like a spoilt child, and the flicker of impatience that scurried across Sebastian's face warned her that that was exactly how he had heard it. He moved with lightning speed across the room, his long, powerful legs eating up the distance between them.

'That's all you ever say, isn't it?' he said as he stood over her. '"I want, I want, I want." Well, from now on, it's what *I* want that matters. You will go to see your father when *I* say, and that won't be till you've fully recovered.'

Kate wanted to cry but she would not give him the satisfaction. Her tears and sorrow were for herself alone. She couldn't speak; she knew her voice would crack, and she had to remain in control—any show of emotion would only be seen as a tantrum by Sebastian, he thought so badly of her.

'Now get back into bed,' he ordered, his voice quieter again, but honed with that sharp edge of authority.

Kate took a deep breath and walked with as much dignity as she could muster. Sebastian followed her wordlessly and lifted the tray from the bed, his eyes scanning the now cold, half-consumed breakfast with disapproval.

'I'll bring you something later,' he told her crisply, and Kate nodded mutely in response. She couldn't answer him—there were no words strong enough to tell him exactly what she thought of him, or how she really felt, but she knew now that the only chance of getting away from him was to do as he asked. Yet she knew he was right—it would do her father's health no good to see her like this.

She couldn't cry; her eyes seemed strangely dry, her mind blank. There was a pain in her chest, a heaviness brought on by worry; she wanted to see her father more than ever now, to be reassured that he was all right. But she would have to wait.

She could telephone, though. The idea brought a smile to her face, and she reached out, snatching the telephone from her bedside table. She repeatedly hit the buttons but the receiver remained silent. Finally, in total frustration, she slammed the receiver down so loudly that she failed to hear Sebastian enter the room again.

'Kate?' he said, looking at her taut, frail figure curled up defensively in her bed, the sheet pulled up high to her chin. Her pale, innocent face looked up at him.

'I want to make a call to my father,' she explained quietly, her expression filled with sadness as she thought he might refuse her request. It had obviously been him on the extension line—he had picked up another telephone in the house to prevent her call from connecting.

'Really?' he said.

'Yes, I do,' insisted Kate, the plea in her voice tangible. She tried to remain impervious to his manner, not wanting to spar with him any more, but she was so keen to hear for herself that her father was all right. 'Can I?'

'Yes,' snapped Sebastian suddenly, a stiff look on his face as he struggled with some inner conflict. Kate guessed that he was wondering whether or not to allow her to make the call. She knew he still did not trust her, but she could also see the human side of him responding to her plea.

'Please, Sebastian,' she begged, and a dark look

passed over his face like a rain-filled cloud crossing an empty sky.

'Yes,' he said finally. 'Of course you can.' He raked his slender, strong fingers through his hair. His dark gaze roamed over her face, but whatever he sought was not there and he mumbled a curse as he turned away. Kate was puzzled by his action; his reactions were far too complicated for her to understand.

She wasted no time. Her fingers rapidly tried the number again and she waited none too patiently as the call went through; the faint ringing was like a nail hammering on her brain till finally she heard the distant voice of her stepmother.

'Hello, it's Kate,' she said breathlessly, a hot stain of colour flooding her ashamed face as she wondered what the other woman's reaction would be. She suddenly felt sick again and knew it was due to nerves; her stomach was a whirl of butterflies. She closed her eyes in relief at her stepmother's words.

'Kate! How utterly marvellous! How are you? It's so good to hear from you. Hold on a minute. I'll get your father.'

Her stepmother's response seemed sincere and Kate felt a twist of remorse. Then she noticed Sebastian, who was watching her reaction with cool interest.

'Daddy,' whispered Kate, her voice barely audible, as if she was afraid to speak any louder. 'Daddy,' she repeated, loving the sound of his name. Knowing that he was able to speak to her was so marvellous. 'How are you?' she breathed, the love she felt for him spilling out without any effort on her part. She could feel hot tears filling her eyes and swallowed hard to try and control the fragile grip she had on her strained emotions. 'Yes, yes, of course. Soon, very soon,' she reassured her father, blinking hard as the silent tears began to trail down her soft cheeks. 'Yes, of course I want to see you. . .' She faltered, the effort of putting joy in her voice becoming too much. 'Yes, of course I do—both of you.'

'It's been such a long time, Kate; you should have been in touch sooner,' her father scolded her, but in a joking manner. Kate was taken aback for a minute. She would have come home at any time but he had totally ignored her. She had received not one reply to the numerous letters she had sent him. Yet now her father seemed to have forgotten all about them, as if the fault lay with her. Maybe it was due to illness or drugs; Kate didn't know, but she was determined to ask him once they were together again.

'I would have come home sooner, Daddy. I just thought. . .' Kate managed to say before her voice began to crack again. Sebastian stared at her, his eyes like cut diamonds, hard and bright. He strode over and took the telephone receiver from Kate's shaky hand.

'Hi, Howard,' he said cheerfully. 'No, she's fine— same as usual,' he told Kate's father, his voice ringing with complete assurance. Kate listened in disbelief. She had changed—why couldn't he see it? Why did he refuse to acknowledge the change in her? she thought furiously as she tried to fathom a reason.

'Yes, she'll be out there by the end of next week. Everything is ticking over. Should be signing contracts with the Duplas Co-operative, but that's not your concern. Yes, that's right.' They talked a little more then Sebastian said, 'Goodbye, Howard.' He replaced the telephone and turned to face the look of fury that was etched on Kate's face.

'Why did you snatch the phone from me?' she demanded, her voice tight with controlled anger. She had so much to say, so much to tell her father, but he had robbed her of that chance. She had to know why her father hadn't replied to her letters, and that she was now truly forgiven.

'Because you were getting over-emotional,' Sebastian informed her crisply.

Kate found that his patronising tone only gave further fuel to her already mounting temper.

'How dare you?' she spluttered. 'There's nothing wrong with emotion. We can't all be as cold-hearted as you,' she spat at him as she drew herself up to face him.

Sebastian took a step closer to the bed and Kate could feel her anger draining away.

'Don't underestimate me, Kate,' he warned her softly. 'Your outburst of emotion may have fooled a frail, ageing man but not me,' he grated nastily.

'What do you mean by that?' Kate protested, her voice shrill with indignation. She hated the insinuation in his words and tone.

'God, you're good,' he mocked, studying her with a cold intelligence. 'Very good,' he crooned. Kate mentally stood her ground. She was not going to be intimidated by him, she told herself repeatedly. 'If I didn't know you better, Kate, you could even fool me with your act of injured outrage.' He raised his hand with deliberate slowness and touched her lips with his strong thumb, stroking it across her mouth. 'But I do know you, Kate. I know all your little games,' he said, shaking his head as if to know her was a mistake indeed. Kate stared up at him, her innocent eyes round, as she struggled to understand the source of his bitterness. 'How clever you are at acting a part. . .' he said. But Kate was not going to remain silent forever. Her sense of pride came to her rescue, and she denied his opinion strongly.

'You're wrong, Sebastian,' she protested hotly, but even as she did so she knew it was pointless. He had a set idea of who she was and nothing was going to change that.

'Am I?' An odd smile touched his lips as his eyes refused to relinquish the hold they had over her. 'I doubt that I haven't worked out just what you're hoping to achieve by this penitent role, but I'll give you fair warning that if you do anything to jeopardise Howard's health you'll certainly pay for it.' He made no attempt to disguise the threat.

Kate turned her head away.

'I'm so glad we understand each other, Kate,' he observed, then turned on his heel and left the room. Kate expelled a huge breath. She had not been aware of how wound up she felt till he had finally gone and now her whole body sagged with relief. She picked up the telephone again. She had to phone Terry, to explain what was happening. He proved to be very understanding, giving her as much time off as she required, and he suggested she visit the Mombasa office while she was away. Kate gladly agreed and replaced the phone with a smile that faded as Sebastian re-entered the room.

'Who were you phoning?' he asked suspiciously, viewing Kate intently, mistrust flaring in his eyes.

'Terry,' she replied airily, noting the play of emotions that scurried over Sebastian's face. 'I needed to speak to him to tell him what was happening.'

'I see,' was the curt response, and Kate could see that he disapproved of Terry.

'Does Daddy still make generous donations to charity?' Kate asked casually enough. She knew what an impact even a small amount could make. The amounts her father had donated in the past could change a community in Africa completely. When her father was fitter, she was determined to get him interested in at least one of her projects.

'Why?' enquired Sebastian dubiously, his stance stiffening slightly as he searched for the reason for her assumed interest. She had always been too self-centred to take an interest in any charity.

'I've a charity he might be interested in,' she said cautiously, sensing Sebastian's doubts. His snort of disbelief confirmed her thoughts.

'Forget it, Kate, there's no way you're having any money. All donations are now made through the company, so there's no way you can just ask Daddy,' he told her firmly.

'I'll still ask him,' she said, not willing to give in so easily. 'I can be very persuasive,' she added, with a smile on her face which she knew would infuriate Sebastian. She was sure her father would be interested in the projects her charity was sponsoring.

'Demanding, you mean,' Sebastian said sharply, and the smile faded instantly from Kate's face. 'Still expect to get everything you ask for?' he added grimly.

'It's not for me,' said Kate indignantly, shifting about in the bed uncomfortably.

'No?' he asked, his eyebrows raising. 'For Terry, then?' he added knowingly.

'Sort of. . .'

'Forget it, Kate; I'm running the company at the moment and I don't feel very charitable towards anything that involves you,' he stated. He left the bedroom, slamming the door behind him.

Over the next few days, Sebastian kept his distance. Kate remained in her room, grateful that his company was not forced on her, yet somehow saddened by the situation. The housekeeper brought her all her meals and Kate could see that she was already gaining a few pounds—it was hard not to when such delicious food was being served. She was feeling much better; the bruising had all but disappeared: it merely looked like shadows around the eyes brought on by lack of sleep.

It came as a surprise to Kate when one morning the housekeeper brought in a neat pile of freshly laundered clothes. She placed them silently on the bed.

Her loyalty to Sebastian was unquestionable so Kate also remained silent, viewing the clothes with mistrust.

'You can get up today,' Sebastian informed her crisply from the bedroom doorway.

'Thanks,' Kate mumbled, carefully avoiding his eyes. There seemed to be little to say to each other any more, as if the years of being apart had made them both forget how close they had been. Now all that was left was a chasm that couldn't be breached.

'We are going shopping,' he informed her.

'We?' echoed Kate, her eyes spinning to his as she tried to decide whether he was joking or not. 'I'm quite capable of choosing my own clothes without your help,' she told him frostily, bristling at the implied criticism.

'That point is debatable.' Sebastian suddenly grinned. 'However, as your car is a write-off, you'll need transport—and I'm hardly likely to let you drive my car,' he added, reminding her of her accident with unnecessary cruelty. However, Kate silently acknowledged the wisdom of that remark; she still was not ready to drive yet, and certainly not a car as large and powerful as Sebastian's top-of-the-range model.

'Besides, I have a couple of appointments in the City,' he continued, taking her silence as agreement.

Though Kate was fuming inwardly at his high-handed attitude, she wasted no time in getting ready. She knew how much Sebastian hated to be kept waiting.

'We'll go to Marshall Square,' Sebastian informed her as he drove them into town.

'No! I don't want to shop there,' she protested. The square was made up of select designer shops.

'Why not?' Sebastian queried, a flicker of understanding flashing across his features. 'Surely you aren't going to persist in refusing to buy some quality clothing?' he said wearily, darting her a quick look before the traffic demanded his attention again.

'Yes. . .no, it's not that. It's just that I no longer feel comfortable in clothes that cost so much. Besides, I like to know where my clothes are made——' she tried to explain, but Sebastian cut in.

'Come off it, Kate,' he said, his mouth twisting with scorn. 'You were always complaining about your allowance. It was never enough. Time and time again you over-spent, and always Howard foolishly gave in to you,' he reminded her. Kate blushed shamefully as she remembered just how selfish she had been. She could remember quite clearly one day when her credit card bill had arrived. She had well exceeded her limit. Her father had been a little angry, but Kate, in her youthfulness, had been quite unrepentant.

'How on earth have you managed to spend so much in one month?' her father had asked incredulously, passing the receipt to Sebastian, who had darted Kate a swift glance of anger as she'd just shrugged indifferently.

'This is a huge amount,' Howard had said, looking at his daughter a little sadly.

'I suppose you resent me spending money, though my own mother would have wanted me to have nice clothes,' she'd complained, knowing how to make her father feel guilty.

'It's not that, Kate——' he began, but she immediately cut in, sensing his weakness and playing on it. What a truculent teenager she had been!

'I never hear you complain about Clare's spending,' she told him tartly, her lips protruding sulkily.

'My mother doesn't over-spend by this amount,' Sebastian said, outraged by her attitude and the insult directed at his mother.

'Mind your own business,' she snapped back. 'I needed those things,' she said dramatically, looking at her father, her eyes pleading. 'Do you want me to look pretty? To have the same things the other girls have?' she asked, her voice soft and charming.

'Of course I do, dear,' answered Howard, unable to resist her sweet, upturned face—and Kate knew it!

'Howard!' put in Sebastian, seeing the outcome of

the conversation. 'Something has to be done,' he reminded him.

'I know, I know,' agreed Howard, then he smiled faintly at his daughter. 'An increase in allowance will help that.'

'That's not the solution,' protested Sebastian, but his objections were drowned under Kate's squeal of delight and she threw a smile of triumph at Sebastian.

'It suits me,' she laughed, and that scene had been played out so many times after that. Kate was always the victor. Sebastian, of course, had more than once jumped in.

'I don't see how this concerns you,' she would throw at him, hoping to silence him.

She always failed.

'Well, this amount does! It's quite ridiculous!'

But that was all in the past. Kate was no longer like that, despite Sebastian's opinion. She shifted uncomfortably in the car seat as she recalled the censure that used to cross Sebastian's face on those occasions.

'No wonder you're so spoilt,' he continued, as if it was an afterthought. Kate remained silent. She knew only too well how badly she had behaved but at the time she had felt it was the only way of getting her father's attention. But that's how he remembers me, she thought sadly, wondering if Sebastian would ever see the change that time had brought about in her.

The car came to a smooth halt, jolting Kate out of her dark memories of the past. She mumbled her thanks as she opened the car door, but Sebastian leant across, taking her arm.

'You'd better take this,' he said abruptly, and he

offered Kate a slim black, leather case with gilt corners. For a moment she was puzzled. She flicked open the case to see a series of credit cards and charge accounts for all the most expensive shops.

'I've had them all made out in your name,' Sebastian said impassively as Kate sat staring at the row of cards, feelng unable to accept them. 'I'm sure that, despite your obvious reluctance,' he continued, 'for your father's sake, you'll force yourself to buy a new wardrobe.'

His words stung Kate because she knew she had no real option but to buy some clothes. But wouldn't that reinforce his low opinion of her? She couldn't win. Kate held down her annoyance as she knew any outburst would be treated with total disdain.

'Remember, hot though Kenya is, you don't own a stitch at the moment.'

'And whose fault is that?' she asked sweetly as she slid from the car. 'Are you sure you can afford this, Sebastian?' she jested, waving the cards under his narrowed gaze. 'You know how much a full wardrobe can cost me.' She laughed as she closed the car door. Sebastian went on to park the car before joining her.

'Where first?' he asked. 'Maybe your hair could do with a trim,' he said critically, rubbing her split ends between his forefinger and thumb. Kate pulled back, annoyed by his action, and the fact he was right.

'Later; now I want to do some clothes shopping,' she said firmly, turning from the square and making her way to the arcade. Sebastian frowned as he followed her.

'You'll be surprised,' she reassured him as she pushed open the door and headed to the nearest shop. The rows and rows of identical skirts and tops

Sebastian viewed with contempt, fingering the cloth with obvious disapproval. Kate ignored him, selecting several skirts and tops, all interchangeable. She then moved on to look at the new summer fashions—brightly coloured T-shirts and shorts and fine summer dresses. Sebastian smiled his approval at a growing pile of clothes that was filling the cash desk.

'Nice to see you haven't lost your old touch,' he commented drily as Kate handed over her card to pay.

'The only difference is these clothes cost a fraction of the price designer labels do. They're just copies. Trust me,' she added, seeing the doubtful expression on his face. Kate's feet were aching. Sebastian was laden down with parcels and she knew she still hadn't bought anything he approved of. He was growing impatient with her. Shopping had never been one of his favourite pastimes, though he was quite fashion-conscious.

'You'll need some beachwear,' he told her, taking the lead this time and escorting her up a narrow street of exclusive boutiques. Kate allowed him to open the door of a tiny shop that specialised in the latest American and Australian beachwear. The selection was tremendous and Kate's attractive and now shapely figure made her able to wear virtually any design. She chose two costumes, holding them up to herself in the mirror.

'Aren't you going to try them on?' chided Sebastian teasingly.

'I don't think that will be necessary—I'm a perfect size twelve,' she flirted back.

'I think you are,' Sebastian agreed, his eyes flicking

wickedly over her body. Kate turned away and busied herself with paying for the items.

'It's a pity you won't see me wearing them, isn't it?' she said teasingly as they left the store. Sebastian turned, a look of puzzlement creasing his brow.

'What on earth makes you think I won't?' he asked, raking a lock of his hair from his face that a sudden gust of wind had blown out of place. Kate froze. Surely he wasn't coming to Kenya? He'd spoil everything, and she couldn't trust herself in his company. She was beginning to realise that he was far too potently attractive for her.

'You're not coming, are you?' she asked incredulously, the thought of him seeing her in that skimpy beachwear alarming her.

'But of course. I couldn't let you travel alone,' he said, putting Kate firmly in her place and reminding her that he still saw her as a child to be looked after. Kate's head tilted back defiantly as she confronted the gleam in his piercing blue eyes, sparing him none of the contempt she felt.

CHAPTER FIVE

KATE lowered her head as she entered the aircraft. The steward smiled warmly at her, extending his hand in greeting. She smiled, then nudged her way down the aisle, following the steward, unaware of the dark thoughts that passed through Sebastian's mind. The steward stood back as he pointed to their seats, his eyes resting on the gentle sway of Kate's hips as she walked down the narrow aisle.

'Do you want the window-seat?' Sebastian said as he took off his jacket and began to fold it up, before giving it to the steward to stow away.

'Thanks,' Kate readily agreed with a nod, shrugging off her own coat and stiffening as she suddenly became aware of Sebastian's strong hands helping her. She fought hard to gain her equilibrium.

'You're looking better,' he acknowledged. 'More yourself,' he added as he sank into the chair next to her, tossing her a careless glance.

'Am I?' said Kate, trying to keep the swell of happiness from her voice and hating herself for seeking his approval. She held his gaze, waiting for him to answer her, her heart beating with a frantic thud against her chest. There was a glitter of warmth in his eyes as he looked at her, studying her with dark intent.

'You know you are; modesty was never one of your strong points,' he reminded her. There was a trace of humour in his voice that Kate was immediately aware of, and she tried to respond to it, to lighten the tension between them and make the long journey more bearable.

'If you've got it, flaunt it,' she laughed. She nodded her thanks to the steward as he turned to attend to some other passengers.

'Behave yourself. We can do without a repetition of your adolescent behaviour,' Sebastian drawled.

His words were like a hard slap and Kate inwardly recoiled. She rested her head back on her seat, closing her eyes. She felt hollow-empty. It seemed that nothing she could do would make up for the past. She had been a fool, she knew that; for example, the series of unsuitable boyfriends she had had were all a desperate attempt to make Sebastian jealous.

Her mind drifted back in time. She had always loved the weekends when Sebastian was home.

Matthew had been the first of many boyfriends whom she had deliberately gone out with to goad Sebastian, hoping to arouse his jealousy.

'I don't want to join you for dinner,' she had told her parents fiercely, her eyes blazing, one Saturday night.

'The table is booked,' Howard reminded her softly.

'So!' said Kate, turning away. 'Who cares?'

'It's supposed to be a family dinner, Kate. Sebastian will be there,' Clare said, hoping to entice her. But Kate remained stubborn.

'A family dinner!' she scoffed, glaring at Clare. 'Matt and I are going to a disco.'

'Can't you go another night?' Clare almost pleaded.

'Why should I?' she snapped back.

'Please, Kate, just for tonight. You can bring Matthew,' pleaded Clare again, but Kate was resolute.

'No, I don't want to.'

She went out that night with Matt, determined to show everyone just how grown-up she was. She arrived back very late and was slightly drunk. She couldn't stop giggling even when Sebastian came out, grabbing her roughly and nearly dragging her inside. He was furious!

'You've been drinking!' he said, quite astonished, his eyes narrowing on her dishevelled appearance. 'What else have you been up to?' he growled.

'Why don't you find yourself a girlfriend, Sebastian, instead of spying on me?' she retorted. Truthfully, she had hated Matt's rough hands on her, greedy and out of control. She had pushed him away, feeling frightened and annoyed, but she wasn't about to tell Sebastian that. She wanted to appear grown-up, mature. 'We were enjoying ourselves, if you must know. You don't know what you're missing,' she laughed, and she hurried upstairs, not waiting to hear his reply.

She regretted that now. It had been futile from the start; no one she loved ever seemed to care for her. She remembered how desolate she had felt when her father's new bride had taken all his attention. Still, she had been determined at that point to be part of her father's life, even if it meant joining the family firm, but when her father had made Sebastian a joint partner in his business that plan had seemed hopeless too. Kate's teeth sank into her bottom lip as she struggled to force her hurt back deep inside.

'You seem nervous, Kate?' Sebastian queried, but

Kate didn't answer. She was back in control now, all her emotions hidden deep away in the dark, safe corners of her mind where no one could reach them.

'Do I?' she replied after a pause, with a fixed smile, her voice surprisingly bright, despite the disturbing shadows in her heart.

'Yes, the thought of playing dutiful daughter face to face, no doubt.'

'No doubt,' Kate agreed quickly, stemming her desire to argue with Sebastian. She shrugged off the feeling, and the subject, with an indifferent air but Sebastian had not finished yet.

'Well, you'd better come up with an Oscar-winning performance—your father is still a very ill man,' he reminded her.

'You think I don't know? Really, Sebastian. . .' she began to protest. His bad opinion of her went too far sometimes and she felt provoked into defending herself at least.

'Cut the righteous indignation, Kate,' Sebastian said, ignoring the stung look on her face. 'Your wide-eyed, innocent look doesn't fool me. I know you too well.'

'People change,' cited Kate, knowing that her words were wasted, and still fighting to try and prove how much she had altered—how much she regretted the past. God knew how many times she had tried to make amends. She just couldn't understand her father's behaviour towards her—it was so out of character.

'Do they?' Sebastian challenged, through her thoughts, the certainty in his voice showing that he thought it was an impossibility. It had always been the same between them—a constant battle of wits—and she was growing tired of it now.

'What's the point of trying to talk to you?' she mumbled, fighting the tension and anger that he could arouse in her with such ease. She was tired of him, fed up with always arguing—couldn't they ever be friends?

'None at all,' he agreed, flashing her a smile of what Kate interpreted as triumph.

'I don't see why you had to come with me. Surely you have more important things to do?' Kate snapped, surprised he had taken the time off from work to accompany her, and troubled because of the unsettling effect he had on her. She wanted so much to show her parents the change in her, but Sebastian seemed ready to goad her at any moment, destroying all her plans for a happy reunion. She noticed an uncharacteristic hesitation before he spoke. He studied her carefully, aware of the fine tension between them. Kate felt forced to meet his gaze head-on to make him realise that in one respect she had changed: she was no longer in awe of him. She now wanted to face him as an equal.

'I'm coming to keep an eye on you,' he admitted honestly. 'Because I know sooner or later this role-playing will become tiresome and you'll revert back to your usual self-centred self.'

'What do you mean by that?' demanded Kate.

'Come off it, Kate. It's all an act; look at that flat— those horrid clothes. I suppose you were hoping that Howard would find you living there with that man so you could pile on the guilt.'

'It wasn't like that,' she denied hotly. What exactly did he think was going on between her and Terry?

Surely he couldn't think they were anything other than friends?' 'It's all I could afford,' Kate protested, hating his assumptions and his unwillingness to listen to her.

'Spare me the details,' he said, waving his hand in dismissal. 'I'm really not that interested.' He pulled his briefcase up on to his lap and flipped it open. Kate stared at him, stung deeply by the things he had said. He always managed to make her feel so bad and for some reason he seemed to take a perverse delight in it.

'I've work to do. It's a long flight and I've these papers to go through before I reach Kenya. You'd best read a magazine or something.' He didn't raise his head from his papers. Kate was incensed; her anger was like a palpable mass, rising within her.

'Just who the hell do you think you're talking to?' she demanded, her anger forcing her voice to a louder than usual pitch, and Sebastian's head came up so quickly that he hit it hard on the open lid of his case.

Serves him right, thought Kate, enjoying the look of pain that flickered across his face as he looked at her. She did not give him a chance to reply before she launched into her attack.

'How dare you dismiss me like that?' she threw at him, her eyes glittering with a silvery brightness. '"Read a magazine!"' She repeated his words, injecting the full contempt she felt for his idea into her tone. 'Women have come out of the kitchen, Sebastian. Why don't you leave the cave and come and join us?'

Kate was breathless when she had finished. Her heart was racing and her cheeks flushed, but enough was enough. After all, it was her father's business as well and she still had a sizeable proportion of shares.

She waited, wondering what his response would be, fully expecting some cutting remark that would silence her.

'I'm sorry, Kate. That was very patronising of me,' Sebastian admitted, and Kate's eyes grew wide in amazement as she saw a flash of admiration in his eyes. 'There's no need to look so surprised. I was in the wrong. I never had any problems with admitting when I've been wrong,' he added, though Kate noted that his apology subtly changed to a gibe at her. He turned his attention back to his papers, a smile teasing the corners of his mouth.

'The business is in Kenya?' asked Kate, unable to keep the surprise from her voice. She still followed the company's plans through the financial papers and had read nothing of a new venture. She watched Sebastian's reaction. His body was suddenly still, quiet, as if he was reluctant to answer her.

'Yes, it is.' His voice was guarded, his tone measured, and Kate knew she would have to ask more questions; he wasn't about to volunteer any information.

'And? Come on, Sebastian,' she cajoled, a thread of anxiety wrapping around her heart as she tried to comprehend his cautiousness. The company had only ever had contracts in Europe. This was a new direction completely.

'It's a new venture, a departure from our usual affairs, but I felt it was time we began to diversify,' he explained as he pulled another sheaf of papers from his case.

Kate felt the familiar wave of jealousy stir within her. She tried hard to expel the doubts that began to creep into her mind, putting them down to her own personal jealousies.

'What exactly is it?' she questioned, part of her always longing to be part of the company her father had built, to know what was going on.

'It's a new project in conjunction with a company already based there. It's not skilled work and the machinery they use does need updating, but I consider it a worthwhile investment,' he informed her as he passed her a copy of his report. His hand touched hers briefly, as lightly as a butterfly's wing, but still Kate's stomach flipped and she pulled her hand back as if she had been pierced by the sharpest of thorns.

'And what does Daddy think?' she asked, her eyes flicking to the papers to cover the depth of emotion that his slight touch had caused.

'I haven't been troubling him with work.'

Kate's head shot back up and she looked at him closely. It seemed impossible to think her father would not be involved; he took his work far too seriously.

'So he doesn't know?' There was an accusation in her tone. The old argument that he wanted to take over the company had been raised even though nothing had been said. They both remembered clearly, so it did not go unnoticed—she felt Sebastian inwardly flinch at her words.

'Yes, of course he knows,' he snapped back, irritated by her familiar lack of trust. 'I'm just not about to worry him over details; besides, it's early days yet,' he explained. 'That's why I have to check over these figures before tomorrow's meeting; then I might have something constructive to tell your father.'

'Can I see? I do know how to read a report,' she said, trying to remain indifferent to his obvious doubts.

'Yes, yes, of course you do. I did expect you to join us,' he replied.

'I wasn't offered a partnership. Remember?' she said stiffly as she took the rest of papers out of his hands.

'Still as bitter as ever, Kate?' Sebastian queried. He seemed unperturbed by her outburst. 'You were eighteen at the time, hardly ready to take on the responsibility of a company partnership.'

The truth of his words pierced deep into Kate's mind, forcing her to reconsider. She had found it hard enough working in a small office, but she wasn't yet prepared to admit that to him.

'Besides,' he continued, gently now, as if he was aware of the fact that his words were touching a nerve, 'at that age you should be out enjoying yourself with people of your own age, not stuck in some smoky boardroom fighting for survival in a very competitive business.'

'But that's what I wanted to do,' protested Kate. She had wanted to be with her father, to be part of his life. She had been tired of being pushed away; had been desperate for his love and attention, which had been denied her for so long.

'Did you really?' Sebastian probed again, his strong hand dropping on to her arm and spreading a warmth throughout her body. Kate swallowed the painful lump in her throat and turned away to concentrate on the papers.

'Are you sure these figures are right?' she questioned him blandly.

'Yes—at least, those were the figures given to me by the Kenya office. Why? Are there some discrepancies?' Steel had re-entered Sebastian's tone and he drew closer to look at the spreadsheets, his musky cologne teasing at Kate's nostrils and weakening her defences against him.

'No, not exactly,' Kate faltered, trying to concentrate while becoming increasingly aware of the slight pressure on her shoulder as Sebastian leaned even further in.

'Come on, Kate,' his voice cajoled, his mouth curling in a teasing smile that made her stomach flip. 'Have you spotted something?' He lowered his head over the spreadsheets, studying them with care. Kate shifted in her chair, sliding to one side in self-protection.

'The estimated payroll seems to be higher than it should be.'

'Does it?' Sebastian's head turned swiftly, his face only inches away from Kate's, and she could feel his warm breath heating her already glowing cheeks. 'How do you know?' he questioned, a frown of interest flickering across his brow.

Kate faltered again. Not yet—she didn't want him to know yet; he would only ridicule her chosen career. She knew the pay for her charity work was poor but the rewards it brought went far beyond the material. She really felt as though she was doing something worthwhile at last. There had been a time when Sebastian had shared those ideals. He too had wanted to change the world. But that was all in the past. He had changed—grown even more cold and cynical.

'Kenya is a relatively poor country, though it fared better than most after it became independent,' Kate began coolly, keeping her secret safe with the change of direction.

'I know.'

'Corruption is widespread. Nepotism on a large scale is the acccepted norm. I think I'd tread very carefully——'

'How come you're such an expert?' Sebastian cut in, an amused grin spreading across his face, and Kate returned his smile with ease. She could actually hear the admiration in his voice.

'I read a lot,' she answered briefly, hoping such an evasive answer would be enough. 'Are you returning to England once your business is complete?' she then asked, steering the conversation on to more neutral ground.

'No, I'll probably take a short break. Louisa will expect it,' he informed her.

'Louisa?' Kate echoed, surprising herself that her voice was so calm when her insides were churning with a full cocktail of emotions as more memories flooded back.

'You remember Louisa?' Sebastian asked squarely. How could Kate forget her—and Sebastian knew that, didn't he? 'When Anne eloped with Frank Myers from Accounts, your father was left high and dry. Luckily enough, Louisa stepped into the breach and she has been there ever since,' he explained.

His response was too pat and that irritated Kate. The very mention of Louisa annoyed her even more when she realised that the girl had become such an integral part of the business that she, Kate, had been denied. There was a lengthy pause as Kate struggled to control her inner feelings and present a façade of indifference.

'How long ago was that?' she asked, intrigued by the changes that had taken place since her departure.

'Shortly after you left, I think,' he answered, quite uninterested. 'Ah, lunch! I'm starved.' He put his papers away and turned his attention to his meal. Kate remained transfixed. She hadn't expected Louisa to be still around and working for her father's company. Surely Sebastian wasn't serious about her? The thought hurt more than Kate wanted to admit even to herself.

'So you're still seeing Louisa?' she asked, trying to sound as casual as possible, hopefully indifferent. Quickly Sebastian fixed a smile on his face, but she noticed it did not extend to his eyes.

'Was I ever?' he said through mouthfuls. 'This isn't bad for airline food,' he added, to encourage her to eat.

Kate sighed inwardly. She knew it was pointless to question him any further—one, because she knew Sebastian would remain evasive, and two, because she did not want to reveal too much interest in his personal life. What had it got to do with her? she questioned herself, and already a niggling doubt was forming in the recesses of her mind, warning her to take care, that she would never be completely over Sebastian.

She was glad when the plane finally touched down. It was great to be back on the ground after such a long flight. The temperature outside was high and the air hot and stifling. A car was waiting for them and within minutes their luggage was loaded and they were driving along the bumpy roads to the family villa. The road was alive with people, and vibrant colours added to the joyous atmosphere. Shops lined both sides of the road and an assortment of local handicrafts hung from every area; bright woven rugs and distinctive animal carvings all jostled beside rolls and rolls of beautifully printed cloths. Children waved as they drove past, shouting, '*Jambo, jambo*,' the Swahili for 'welcome', and ran for a short time after the car in the hope of a few coins or sweets being tossed to them.

'It's as beautiful as ever,' whispered Kate as she absorbed the atmosphere, enjoying the colourful scenes that passed before her eyes. 'Like paradise,' she added as an afterthought just as the clear blue coastline came into view.

'Let's hope there's no serpent in the garden this time,' remarked Sebastian, his eyes remaining firmly fixed on the road ahead.

'I suppose you're referring to me.' Kate felt her temper rising once more and tried to control it.

'If the cap fits. . .' began Sebastian, but he didn't bother to finish the well-known phrase as he heard Kate's sudden intake of breath. A low white bungalow had come into view. Kate felt a tightness in her chest at the sight of the family villa where she had spent so many happy holidays. She felt a hot sting of unshed tears sear the back of her eyes, filling them with the glint of sorrow. Sebastian drew the car to a smooth halt and Kate sat immobile as she took in the fresh scent of the flowers, the glorious garden that was filled with bright bougainvillaea, fragrant frangipani and the vivid blooms of the hibiscus. Suddenly she felt afraid. Sebastian turned but she was barely aware of his action till he touched her arm, breaking into her reverie. She turned and looked at him, her eyes wide with fear and softened by the tears. She didn't speak; emotion momentarily robbed her of the power of speech. For an unbearably long second there was only silence, then Sebastian placed his hand comfortingly over hers. His long fingers closed around hers till her small hand was lost in his strong hold. She looked at him, her pulse quickening at the tender look that rose in the dark depths of his eyes.

'I'm scared, Sebastian,' she admitted, thinking of the reunion she was about to face. 'I don't think I can go through with it.'

'You'll be all right,' he reassured her, his fingers applying a slight pressure to hers as he spoke, as if trying to share his own strength with her. A faint tremor quivered through Kate at the excitement his touch ignited in her. He released her fingers slowly, allowing Kate time to steady her racing pulse.

He opened the car door. 'Come on,' he said encouragingly. She looked up, feeling a warm tingle sweep over her as he helped her from the small Jeep. She hesitated, but at that moment the ebony wood door of the villa opened and she heard a familiar voice call.

'Kate!'

Then words and actions happened simultaneously, the depth of her emotion threatening to overwhelm her.

'Daddy!' she cried, forgetting everyone as she rushed towards him, her love blocking out everything else. The tears that she had fought so hard to control now flowed freely without her even being aware of them. She flung her arms around her father, hating the uncharacteristic fragility she felt in his frame and yet still clinging to it and seeking the comfort and security she longed to find there. 'Daddy.' She whispered his name again as if it were an incantation as she planted a kiss on his cheek, her arms wrapping tightly around his chest as she held on to him, squeezing him till she took his breath away. She felt his arms around her, too, the familiar, reassuring arms that had held her when she was a child.

'You're looking well,' she managed, wiping the back of her hand across her cheeks to remove a damp patch of tears. Their hands were still linked and she rejoiced in the feel of her father's hand in hers; it was so natural, so perfect that it seemed odd he had refused to have her home, ignored her pleas for forgiveness.

'Well?' Howard said as he looked at his daughter thoughtfully.

'You're looking better than I thought you would,' Kate admitted, with a smile that sprang naturally to her lips. It was so good to see him again.

'Clare's been taking good care of me,' Howard agreed, wrapping his arm affectionately around his wife's waist as she came to join them. Clare responded by resting back against her husband, their mutual love for each other apparent in their actions, which made Kate feel slightly ill at ease.

'I'm sure she has,' Kate said a little icily, ignoring Clare completely. Kate knew she had changed little in that respect; even though she was no longer as jealous of Clare as she had been she still felt a stab of anger at her presence.

'Come on, I've already fixed the drinks,' offered Clare as they moved into the cool hall. The sound of footsteps tapping on the cold ceramic tiles stopped them and Kate stared at her old adversary with the familiar feelings rising up within her. Louisa effectively ignored Kate, merely nodding to the whole family, while she directed all her attention on Sebastian.

'Sebastian,' she said, her voice husky and low. 'It's lovely to see you. I see you found Kate, but do you think it was wise bringing her here?'

Kate felt a surge of feeling and clamped down on it with a sudden fierceness. She was here to make amends, to repair any damage she had done, not to clash with everyone again. She tried to close her ears to Sebastian's reply as she followed her parents into the large lounge but she caught him saying, 'Don't worry, Louisa, I'll be keeping a close eye on her. Besides. . .'

Kate could not bear to hear any more. What had she expected—the red carpet to be thrown out in welcome? She knew it was going to be hard but was determined to show them all how much she had changed. She took the long iced drink Clare offered her with a forced smile, then sank on to the floor next to her father's chair, resting her head on his legs as she looked up at him, hating the signs of old age she saw in his face. He reached out, placing his hand on her head, stroking her hair.

'It's good to have you back, Kate. We have all missed you,' he said, with a reassuring smile.

'I'm glad to be back. I would have come back sooner. . .' she began, but, despite the desire that sprang up inside her to ask him why he had refused to see her before now, she trailed off into silence. Suddenly it seemed pointless. The important thing was that they were back together again. She rested her head back, closing her eyes as she wallowed in the luxury of being with her father again and feeling the soothing touch of his hand.

'How touching.'

Kate's eyes flew open at the velvet taunt of Sebastian's voice. She felt uneasy under his contemplative gaze but forced a smile on her face, ignoring his barb.

'Come on, Kate,' Sebastian continued. 'I'd like to show you the new pool we've had put in.'

It was a polite enough invitation but Kate knew it was an offer she would be foolish to ignore. Besides, she could feel the burning-hot wrath of Louisa upon her and that acted like a catalyst. She jumped to her feet, feigning delight.

'I'll be back in a minute,' she said to her father, planting an affectionate kiss on his cheek. He responded with another indulgent smile.

'You certainly have fooled Howard, maybe even my mother, but remember, Kate, you'll never fool me,' Sebastian warned, once they were outside. Kate picked carelessly at one of the flowers that hung down from the beams forming the pergola to try and cover her awkwardness.

'It's not an act,' she said defensively.

'Isn't it?'

Kate stiffened at the challenging tone of his voice and tipped her head back to look at him. No matter how hard she tried, her pride would not give in to him. She recalled the carefully rehearsed phrases that she knew would antagonise him.

'I can understand your concern; you might have to share your half of the company.' She smiled sweetly as she spoke but Sebastian remained impassive to her words, and his complacency only served to fire her anger. She saw the knowing look in his eyes as he stared at her and her heart sank. It still hurt her to think that he thought so badly of her.

'I'd be careful, Sebastian,' she continued bravely, still wanting to annoy him, to hurt him as much as his indifference hurt her. 'Who knows what might happen now I've returned?'

'Nothing,' he said evenly. 'Nothing at all will happen, Kate, so don't waste any time making futile plans. You're here to help in your father's recuperation, and once you stop doing that I'll take you right back to England.'

'No, Sebastian. I'm not going anywhere till I'm ready, and I do what I want,' she said, standing up to him.

'Oh, don't we all know it?' he drawled at her.

'What do you mean by that?' Kate demanded, hating the indifference in his tone and the superior look on his face.

'You've always had exactly what you wanted. I remember when Howard couldn't go to America because you made such a fuss.' She could see the bitterness as black as coffee in his vivid eyes.

'He didn't want to go,' she protested.

'Of course he did. He was proud of my success but you resented any attention that wasn't given wholly to you,' Sebastian told her, sparing her none of his contempt.

'That's not true!'

'You know damned well it is! Your only motivation is the fulfilment of your own desires. I know why you're being kind to Howard—it's because you want money!'

'It's for charity,' she said angrily, hating his accusation; it was so untrue—so unfair.

'I don't care what it's for. Howard is not to be bothered. You just watch your step,' he warned, before adding, 'And do try to treat my mother with a little respect.'

Kate remained stubbornly silent. She felt strangled by the anger that squeezed her dry throat. She raised her face, her gaze falling on his ruthless features, and she knew he meant every word.

'Understand?' he said. He took hold of her arm. Kate glared at him as she struggled briefly, trying to shake off the firm grip he had her trapped in, but he wouldn't let go and she was forced to stand there and face him.

'Kate?'

'Yes, yes, I understand,' she bit out, her whole body shaking. 'You lost your father because your mother saw mine as a better catch, and you want my father as a substitute!'

Cursing under his breath, Sebastian's grip tightened still further.

'One of these days, Kate——' he ground out between his tightly clamped jaws and, despite Kate's angry struggle, she was trapped, locked in his arms, unable to prevent him from kissing her. Kate could remember Sebastian's kisses only too well. They were warm, soft, full of love and passion, not like this onslaught, which was bereft of any tenderness. She forced herself to hate him, to ignore the rapid tattoo her pulse was drilling through her body. He dragged his mouth across her blazing cheeks.

'Kate,' he murmured thickly, his lips still against her face. 'Why do you do this to me? Why?'

His hand went instinctively to her lips and he traced their softness, ignoring her feeble protests. Kate pulled away. Her body was growing weaker but she couldn't allow herself to be fooled by him again. She pushed him right away, breaking free, and looked him straight in the eye.

'Stay away from me, Sebastian,' she stated. She knew how weak her protest sounded and she caught the laughter in his eyes as he moved away.

'I can't do that, Kate. You see, I don't trust your motives,' he told her. 'So, much as I'd like to stay away from you, I'm afraid I simply cannot.' The flash of white teeth denoted a smile but there was no warmth or laughter in it. He then spun round quickly and walked away.

'Sebastian,' Kate called after him, and there was a slight pause in his stride, so Kate knew he had heard her, but he carried on walking.

CHAPTER SIX

KATE was grateful for the heavy workload Sebastian seemed to have—it kept him so busy that she rarely saw him except at mealtimes—and, as all the family was there, no one seemed to notice the strained atmosphere between them, or their lack of conversation with each other. Kate longed to take over the care of her father but it was a constant source of friction between her and Clare, who had taken total responsibility for her husband since his heart attack.

'I'll see to that, Clare,' Kate said one afternoon, getting to her feet to make her father some tea.

'No sugar now, and half-fat milk,' Clare reminded her gently, annoying Kate more than she realised.

'I know,' Kate snapped back, then added, 'Why don't you go and rest, Clare?'

'I can't,' she answered, then caught Kate's expression. 'Honestly, Kate, I can't,' she sighed.

'You mean won't! What do you think I'm going to say to him? Something awful to bring on a relapse?' Kate asked, hurt by her stepmother's attitude.

'Perhaps not purposefully, Kate, but. . .' Clare's voice trailed away.

'I haven't come here to argue, or to rake up the past,' Kate explained. Then she added painfully, 'Why can't you believe that?'

'I'm sorry, Kate. It's just that I'm frightened.'

'Frightened?'

'Yes. When I came close to losing Howard, I was devastated. I'm scared of leaving him alone in case. . .' But Clare was unable to finish the sentence.

'I see,' acknowledged Kate, suddenly seeing her stepmother as a frail older woman who was in need of a good rest. 'Trust me, Clare, I'll look after him,' she reassured her. Clare faltered for a moment, then a soft smile lit her worn face.

'Thanks, Kate,' she nodded.

Though Kate had willingly taken charge of him, she thought it would be no easy task, as Howard Peterson was a true workaholic and was never really happy unless absorbed in some deal or other. But as it happened they had so much catching up to do that, for once in his life, Howard Peterson forgot all about work. Many times Kate wanted to question him, to ask him why he had sent back her letters and cards, but somehow she felt that mentioning the past might jeopardise the easy relationship that was developing between them now. Kate wasn't prepared to take the risk. She tried to suffocate her natural curiosity and concentrate instead on the friendship that they had. She was pleased, too, that Clare had moved aside, giving them both time together, so that Kate was forced to look at her stepmother in a new light. It was obvious that Clare cared deeply about her husband and was willing to do anything to make him happy.

Kate was into the second week of her holiday when she came down to breakfast one morning to find her father engrossed in conversation with Sebastian.

'I think Kate deserves a rest.' Howard paused as she entered, and Kate gave him an affectionate peck on the cheek before sliding into the white cane chair next to him and resting her hand over his. 'She has been looking after me non-stop since she arrived, but of course she has her accident to recover from as well,' he continued, the delight in his voice making Kate's heart soar with joy. Her eyes darted to Sebastian, who studied her suspiciously before turning his attention back to Howard. Kate, conscious of his glance, shifted uncomfortably in her chair. She began to pour herself a coffee, her hand shaking just a little.

'Clare has been grateful for the break and we really enjoy both of you being here, but it would be nice——' Howard never managed to finish his sentence as Sebastian cut in,

'To have some time alone.'

'Exactly. Louisa is taking a few days off, so you could take Kate out for some sightseeing.'

Kate flushed with embarrassment at Sebastian's reluctance. Howard had obviously been trying to persuade him to escort Kate for the day and, as Sebastian was not forthcoming, she felt mortified.

'Really, Daddy, you make me sound like a child. I'm more than capable of occupying myself for the day,' she said quickly, in an attempt to cover the embarrassing silence. Sebastian's eyebrows rose at her words and he held up his hands in a sign of defeat, a smile teasing the corners of his mouth.

'I give in. I'll take a day off, he said, his voice lacking any real enthusiasm. Kate slammed her coffee-cup back into its saucer, spilling the contents.

'That won't be necessary, Sebastian. I had planned on having a day on the beach,' she said, pushing her chair back as she stood to leave, longing to be out of his presence. There was something about him that seemed constantly to antagonise her.

'And I know just the place,' Sebastian said firmly, startling Kate into further defiance.

'I'd rather spend the day on my own,' she snapped, rigid with tension.

'Now, now, Katy,' admonished Sebastian, using her childhood name and mockingly wagging his finger at her. 'That's no way to behave when I'm offering to take you out for the day,' he teased. A tint of colour stained Kate's cheeks as she looked at him, but she was unable to suppress a smile that tugged at the corners of her mouth. She shook her head.

'Are you sure?' she asked, a trace of doubt in her voice as she looked at him, but already feeling a little excited at the prospect.

'Of course,' he drawled lazily. 'I've something really special in mind,' he added mysteriously with a wink, his expression softer and inviting, and Kate felt her stomach contract. She felt she had been stabbed. The intense longing for him was a real physical pain and she hated the way she reacted to him. Determined not to allow Sebastian to know how she felt, she gathered herself together, hiding her turmoil behind a façade of indifference. She needed her protective armour intact if she was to spend the day with him—she knew exactly how potent Sebastian's charm could be.

'All right,' she said coolly, moving past him, and as she did so he touched her. She stopped, frozen to the spot, the familiar gesture of his hand resting gently on her arm increasing the flow of blood through her body.

'I shall ask Jasmine to fix us a picnic. I'm sure she'll oblige.'

'No doubt she will,' answered Kate, moving away. Jasmine, the local woman who came in as a daily help, like all women, was not immune to Sebastian's charm. He grinned as if he knew what she was thinking.

'Can you be ready in thirty minutes?' he asked.

'No problem.'

'Good. If I'm to take a day off, I don't want to waste a minute.'

'Nor me,' agreed Kate, blowing a kiss at her father as she scurried from the room. She suddenly felt light-hearted, happier than she had been for months.

A day on the beach certainly required a change of clothing and Kate felt suddenly grateful that Sebastian had made her buy some new clothes. She realised now that perhaps her views had been a little extreme at first. She had felt so guilty about her lifestyle when she had first begun to work for the Third World charity that she had deliberately toned down her wardrobe, and her small wage had made re-stocking it with expensive designer clothes an impossibility. So she took an extra delight in her new outfits.

Over one of her new swimsuits she slipped a smart pair of orange-toned shorts, matched with a colourful jungle-print T-shirt, and slid her feet into a pair of slim golden sandals. She had already achieved a golden tan as she had carefully sunbathed every afternoon when her father had been resting. She grabbed a large shoulder-bag from the top of the wardrobe and hurriedly began to fill it with her other swimsuit, very fashionably cut high on the leg, a thick, colourful beach-towel and an assortment of sun lotions.

Kate grinned when she remembered something else she had brought. She sat on the bed, blowing hard at an inflatable ring. It was shaped like a dolphin and had two beautiful blue eyes that rattled. Kate knew it would appeal to Sebastian's wacky sense of humour.

She hauled her bag on to her shoulder and, tucking the dolphin under her arm, glanced at her reflection as she passed the mirror. She looked young—very young. Her blonde hair had lightened in the sun and her heavy fringe hung over her dove-grey eyes—she looked like an innocent teenager! She paused for a moment, scooping her hair from her shoulders and holding it up on top of her head; she turned her face from side to side as she tried to decide whether to put it up—to do that would certainly make her look older. Then she released it; she preferred it loose. Besides, Sebastian wouldn't notice either way. Not that she wanted him to, she reminded herself as she opened the bedroom door, her heartbeat already increasing.

'Kate,' purred Louisa, who was passing by her room, 'you look lovely—so sweet.' Her voice was thick and honey-coated but it did not conceal the underlying venom that Kate disntinctly heard. 'Quite the young lady,' Louisa added, with a smile fixed on her face. Kate tried to return the smile but failed. She felt such a fool. Louisa was everything she was not: she was dressed in a taupe linen suit, a thin white silk camisole that matched her pair of low-heeled, peep-toed shoes and a wide white belt that emphasised her slender waist. Her hair was carefully arranged in a sophisti-cated chignon and her make-up was perfectly applied. Despite the heat, she showed no signs of distress, though beads of perspiration were already making Kate's face glow.

'Is that a new toy?' Louisa asked slightly scornfully,

her perfectly shaped eyebrows rising in amusement. Kate pulled her inflatable dolphin closer to her and, despite Louisa's attempt to ridicule her, she managed to laugh.

'Oh, you mean Danny?'

'Danny?' asked Sebastian, coming up behind them. It was the first time he had intervened between the two ladies since Kate had arrived. It was as if he was enjoying the barbed comments.

'Danny Dolphin.'

'I should have guessed,' laughed Sebastian, obviously recalling how Kate always named her toys. 'Like Freddy Fox, Bobby Bear and Porky Pig?'

'Percy Pig,' Kate corrected him, enjoying the shared moment of intimacy, a memory from childhood which effectively shut out Louisa and which, for some reason that Kate was not going to think about, she deeply delighted in. She knew Louisa was stinging from her exclusion—she could see it in the tension lines that pulled at the girl's mouth and her sullen expression.

They walked downstairs and out to Sebastian's car. Kate climbed into the back and leant forward, pushing her head between Louisa and Sebastian, who sat in front, in a pretence of wanting to talk.

'It's good of Sebastian to look after you today. I'm sure your father will want your company again soon,' Louisa said in a consolatory tone. Kate immediately sank back as if she had been slapped. Had her father tired of her? Did he no longer want her company? She remained silent, stunned by Louisa's words but knowing them to be the truth. It was always the same: Howard soon tired of her, always had done, and the familiar feeling of rejection welled up inside her like a huge wave of water beating against a dam. Kate stared out of the window, ignoring the careless chatter of Louisa. She was too lost in her own thoughts, her own bitter pain twisting inside her. She hardly noticed the car drawing to a halt, or Louisa alighting, but she was aware of the kiss that Louisa gave Sebastian. Kate's nerves tensed at the sight of it but she refused to acknowledge the jealousy that stirred deep within her.

'Come and sit up front, Kate. You'll get a better view,' Sebastian said as they set off again, and Kate did not need a second invitation. She scrambled over the seat and settled herself down next to Sebastian.

'Where exactly are we going?'

'Nylia Beach.'

Kate nodded, but she was not prepared, despite her high expectations, for the beauty that was awaiting her. The beach was an endless stretch of pure white sand that shimmered with a silvery light. The sea was a clear deep blue and as smooth and flat as a fine sheet of glass.

Sebastian parked the car in the rough car-park in the harbour, leaving Kate alone for a few minutes. She waited, enjoying the lovely view and listening to the gentle lapping of the water on the shore.

'It's all fixed.'

'What is?' asked Kate.

'I've booked us on to a boat trip, to see the reef. I thought you might like to go diving,' Sebastian explained, misinterpreting her silence as unwillingness to go.

'Diving?' she whispered. 'It's been years,' she said wistfully, recalling the time when he had first taught her to scuba. It had been a family holiday in the

Caribbean, one of the happiest, but it was after then that her relationship with Sebastian had begun to change. It was not as easygoing as it had been after that; there was a strain there that she couldn't comprehend.

'So are you interested?' snapped Sebastian irritably.

'Of course,' breathed Kate. The thought of seeing the reef filling her mind, she followed Sebastian to the tiny hire shop, where she opted for a sleek black wet suit emblazoned with a fluorescent band of orange down the full length of each side. Then, within moments, they were boarding a boat and setting sail.

'Ready?' asked Sebastian a short time later as he studied her perched on the edge of the boat, her hands wrapped around the edge as she leant back. Kate avoided looking at him directly; she could remember clearly how stunning he would look in a wet suit. The tight fit covered his body, emphasising the sleek strength of his male frame. She nodded and took a deep breath, hesitating for a moment as a niggle of apprehension filtered through her mind. But she heard the splash of water behind her and that was invitation enough.

Without any further doubts, she released her grip, leant back and slipped into the calm, warm waters. She could feel the weight of the sea pressing hard against her as she sank beneath the waves, swimming lower and lower. She followed the supple body of Sebastian as he swept further down. Nothing could have prepared Kate for the wonderful sight before her; she turned in astonishment to Sebastian, her eyes dancing with unspoken delight. The reef was alive with activity: summer was drawing to a close and the coral was spawning. The clear blue water changed to a cloudier green, thick with the millions upon millions of tiny egg-packets. Kate watched in fascination as the tiny balloons swelled up from the coral before bursting and releasing in the water. Worms began to emerge, intertwining their green and blue and red strands into the rose-coloured spawn.

Kate was far too engrossed in the miniature life forms in front of her to notice the dark shadow that was cutting silently through the water. She was oblivious to the slow beat of a fish tail as the whale-shark approached. Her breath caught in her throat as Sebastian suddenly drew her in towards him and her heart skipped a beat, but the intent look in his eyes warned her that all was not right. Her own eyes darted about, trying to focus on the danger: the sea was always full of it and she knew that something was wrong! The power of Sebastian's action had alerted her; her back was pressed up hard on to his chest and he wrapped his arms protectively around her tense body as he drew her back into the large rocks. The shadow of the huge fish cast its darkness over them and Kate shut her eyes momentarily. It was young, about twenty feet long, its eyes ebony jewels, its teeth large white pyramids of power and strength. Kate's heart tightened at the awesome sight, her stomach churning as she considered the danger they were in, yet strangely enough the reassuring presence of Sebastian helped her to release the tension in her chest and breathe.

The shark passed them, close enough for them to see the clear design on its back: a spectacular colour-pattern of white polka dots on a rich navy background.

It moved gracefully, sinking lower and deeper into the water, and Kate watched its descent until she could see it no more. Sebastian did not release her instantly, though the strength of his grip slackened. Kate felt herself being cradled protectively in his arms and she allowed herself a moment of self-indulgence, moving her body closer to his. She turned her head, tilting it upwards so that she could see his face. His dark eyes were visible through the face-mask, staring at her with an intensity that she found strangely disturbing. Then she saw the change, a flicker of something—it was far too quick for her to define what it was—but Sebastian's reaction was instant. His arms dropped and then Kate felt a sharp shove on her shoulder as he pushed her away and indicated that they should reach the surface quickly. Kate did not need to be told a second time. The magic of the moment had been lost and destroyed forever. She floated away, glad of her face-mask. She began to kick herself upwards, making for the surface, her legs moving frantically as she tried to escape. But she couldn't help but wonder who she considered the real threat—Sebastian or the shark! She splashed to the surface, pulling away her mask and breathing fresh air with relief. Sebastian rose at the side of her and removed his mouthpiece to speak.

'That was exciting,' he said, pushing his mask up on to his forehead. 'They don't normally come this early on. It follows a pattern: first the coral spawns, attracting the smaller fish, then the food chain continues till the whale-sharks arrive, but usually not for another few weeks.'

Kate was glad of his enthusiasm as it allowed her to

recover her equilibrium. She kicked her legs gently, keeping herself afloat as she listened to him.

'I wish we'd had a camera—what a shot!'

'Aren't they dangerous, sharks?' Kate commented, her heart still thudding as she recalled the size of the beast.

'It's hard to say. Some fishermen claim their boats are attacked but I doubt that's the case. You see, they eat by sifting the water through their mouths. If a boat happens to be in the same area fishing, it might look as if the shark is attacking them, open-jawed and hungry, but I doubt it. Anyhow—whale-sharks especially are generally harmless—you just need to be careful because of their size! He laughed as he lay back in the water, but Kate was not amused. She began to climb up the side of the boat with sharp, quick movements.

'Hey, what's the matter, Kate?' Sebastian called after her, scrambling to her side and meeting her on the deck, a pool of water forming at their feet. 'You weren't frightened, were you?' he asked, sounding almost concerned, but she could hear the laughter in his voice, too.

'Yes, I was,' she snapped back. 'Very frightened.'

'You have no need, Kate,' he said, his voice softer now and as warm as the sweet air that teased her damp hair from her face. 'You should know I'd never let anything harm you.'

The words hung in the air between them, sounding oddly poignant. Kate nodded silently, hating the hopes and desires his words created. She hurried away, leaving him standing alone on the deck, lost in his own thoughts. She could feel his eyes still following her and sensed his confusion, but the situation was impossible. He did care for her—he always had done—but not in the way she wanted. He saw her as a little sister in need of protection and Kate was no longer sure what she felt for him. Her emotions swung so erratically, it was impossible for her to know exactly how she felt.

She took longer than she needed to dress, her mind still racing with a mixture of thoughts and emotions, and it was with reluctance that she joined Sebastian back on the deck. He stood leaning against the rail and gazing into the bottom of the boat, which had a window into the sea. Kate watched him, noting his total absorption in the changing picture of underwater life, his eyes and mind lost in the sea world. He had changed, too, and was now wearing a pair of dark navy shorts and a slim-fitting white T-shirt. He looked so relaxed, not in the least bit threatening, but Kate was not about to drop her guard. She knew love could cause as much pain as it did pleasure, and she wasn't about to take the risk. If only she could look upon him as a brother and nothing more. She had to—anything else was a waste of time and bound to end in tears. . .

She took a steadying breath and braced herself. He's my stepbrother, my stepbrother, she chanted over and over in her head as she approached. She stood by his side, their arms touching briefly.

'Are you OK now?' he asked, glancing up briefly before returning his attention to the sea.

'Yeah, fine. It was just the shock, that's all,' she lied convincingly. 'Still, something to tell the grand-children.' She managed a stiff smile.

'You're planning on having children, then?'

'Some day—and you?'

'I guess.'

Covertly she studied the sharp angles of his face, so hard and unyielding. 'Do you think you'd make a good father, Sebastian?' she asked, unable to keep the doubt from her voice.

'You don't, I presume?' he asked as he swung round. She could read the tell-tale signs of his anger behind his swift movements. It was the way his eyes gleamed with a spark of indignation that could ignite his temper at any moment. Kate remained silent but the expressive shrug of her shoulders told him all he needed to know.

'I won't be like your father, if that's who you're comparing me to,' he told her, and in that instant her own anger was aroused.

'My father is an excellent man and he has been a good father to you,' she bit back, angered by his criticism of a man who had shared his home, life and love with another man's child.

'To me, yes, but what about you, Kate?' he asked, his words smooth but probing. 'I was already fully grown when I met your father, but you——'

'He's always given me everything I ever wanted,' she cut in desperately, while a tormenting voice whispered in her ear, Except love, Kate, never love.

'Yes, well, that was his mistake; that's why you're so spoilt,' Sebastian concluded matter-of-factly.

Kate's hand tightened around the boat's rail and she fixed her sight on it. 'Sebastian——' she began, her voice grating.

'I'm sorry, Kate, but that's the truth,' he interrupted her, suddenly impatient as he swung away and headed for the rear of the boat—as if tired of the conversation.

Kate went after him, her muscles tight with indignation.

'I'm spoilt?' she said to him through gritted teeth, hurt that he should see her needs so easily filled by material wealth. Her father had given her everything but love.

'That's right.' He pivoted round.

'I had everything, did I?' she asked sarcastically. Her father had given her everything. 'Everything money could buy,' she continued bitterly, but Sebastian stopped her.

'We're not playing the role of poor little rich girl, are we, Kate?'

He laughed without humour.

'I only ever wanted one thing, Sebastian, and you took that,' she told him, her eyes fixed on his in confrontation. 'You robbed me of my partnership in my father's company.'

'That's not true, Kate,' he said, shocked. 'You know it isn't.'

'Not true!' Kate scoffed. 'Then how come you have the partnership and I don't? she challenged.

'Because you were too young, too selfish and too spoilt. You weren't ready to work hard and you just couldn't bear the thought that someone had something you didn't,' he told her.

'Thief!' she spat at him, shaking her head as she swallowed the taste of envy, sour memories flooding her mind. But it was all in the past now. She realised that she had been too young to take up a serious role in the company. Besides, these days she was far happier working for her favourite charity. She derived a satisfaction from knowing that she had helped people in a positive way, rather than being part of a large corporation. If only she could explain all this to Sebastian, and make him understand, but she knew that he would only twist what she had to say and they would end up arguing as usual. In that respect they *were* like siblings—he always teasing and both of them forever fighting. Kate, though, was battle-weary, and longed to achieve the same peace and understanding with Sebastian that she now had with her father.

She glanced round, looking for him. He was standing looking out across the clear blue sea as if searching for a lost island. She joined him, standing silently at his side. He reminded her of the sea: deep and vast, with hidden dangers as well as hidden treasures. Then he turned, the sunlight shining on his face, lighting the fine lines around his eyes. He smiled, his teeth bright white in the daylight.

'I'm sorry, Kate, I shouldn't have said that.' He swung away and settled himself on a deckchair. Kate followed him, sitting down next to him.

'You're right, Sebastian, I was spoilt,' she admitted, still keeping some of her thoughts to herself. She wanted his understanding without being forced into giving him explanations.

'Yes, but you were cute with it,' he grinned.

'Was I?' she asked, wrapping her arms around her hunched-up legs and hugging them, despite the heat of the day.

'Yes, very,' he acknowledged. 'It would be hard not to spoil a child if she was as cute as you were,' he added with a touch of humour and a hint of understanding.

'What's with the past tense? I'm still cute,' Kate

mock-objected, turning to smile at him, but there was a far-away look in his eyes, a lost, haunted expression that made her smile stiffen and freeze on her lips. She knew that at that moment he was thinking of long ago. Back to the times when they had been inseparable. The past had forced its way into the present, sending a flurry of shared images racing through their minds. It was too dangerous and Kate moved swiftly away.

'I think the boat is about to stop. Where are we?' she asked, steering the conversation back to the safe present. Sebastian stood as the boat rocked to a stop, his eyes scanning the area.

'Picnic time,' he said, a forced lightness in his voice as he strode away to reclaim their supplies. Kate waited, watching him, conscious of the awkwardness and tension that had sprung between them once more.

CHAPTER SEVEN

SEBASTIAN placed the ice-box on the shore before
returning to collect Kate. He reached his arms out to
her.

'Come on, Kate,' he grinned, sensing her reluctance.
'I promise I won't drop you.'

'You'd better not,' she agreed, falling into his outstretched arms and holding herself rigid. She could
feel the supple movements of his chest muscles as he
picked her up and strode to the beach, the gentle play
of his muscles under his shirt rippling against her own
soft body. Kate was pleased when that ordeal was over
and he placed her on the sand.

'Delivered safely,' he said triumphantly. Kate
walked away and settled herself on the hot, soft white
sand. There was a hidden bond that welded them
together in a special way. She picked up a handful of
sand and allowed it to trail through her fingers.

'It's lovely and quiet here,' she said as Sebastian
joined her, flopping down next to her with a casual
air.

'I'm going to do some serious sunbathing. This is my
first day off since arriving here,' he confessed as he
pulled his T-shirt up over his shoulders. Kate lowered
her head and cast a covert glance under her eyelids.
His physique was as powerful as ever. His chest was
strong, with well-defined pectorals, and he had a rigid
flat stomach. She saw his fingers catch hold of the

button of his shorts and twist it unfastened. She looked out to sea, concentrating on the lace-edged waves that lapped quietly on to the silver sand.

'Did you pack any oil?' he asked as he sank back on to the sand, his dark eyes skimming over her as she continued to stare out to sea. 'Kate?'

'Yes—yes, of course. It's in here somewhere,' she murmured, and dived into the depths of her bag, searching for the elusive sun oil. 'Here,' she said, offering the bottle to Sebastian but keeping her eyes firmly on the ground.

'No, you do it,' he drawled lazily, lying on his stomach and propping his head up on his elbows.

Kate froze. Her hands were hot and clammy with the beads of sweat that had broken out across her palms. She looked at the expanse of his back, his shoulders firm and glistening in the sunshine, broad and rigid.

'Come on, Kate, I can already feel the heat,' he complained, his eyes closed and unable to read her hesitation. She opened the top of the oil and trickled it down the ridge in his spine, watching the golden liquid descend till it dampened the top of his trunks.

'Mmm, this is the life,' said Sebastian, shifting in the sand. His movements shocked Kate into action. Bracing herself, she placed her palms on his shoulders and began a slow and methodical massage. She could feel the tension in his body begin to ebb slowly away and it gave her an impetus. She sank her fingers deeper into his warm flesh and enjoyed the soft groan that escaped from his lips. Her fingers grew stronger and she began to enjoy the feel of his skin next to hers. She stroked the oil across his back till it gleamed. Then

Kate hesitated. She moved her hand down lower till she was close to the edge of his trunks. She paused as she felt the tension return swiftly to Sebastian's body; there was a sudden tightness she had not expected.

'There,' she said, glad it was over but not questioning herself too much on why that should be. Sebastian had opened his eyes; they looked sleepy but knowing. He looked at her for a long, uncomfortable moment before speaking.

'Haven't you a swimsuit with you?' The corners of his mouth curled into a delicious, sensuous smile that was warm with a dangerous invitation. Kate nodded as her skin-tone pinkened.

'Underneath my shorts and T-shirt.'

'Well, go on, then,' he said, closing his eyes again, totally relaxed as the hot sun washed over his body.

'I'll set the picnic up first,' Kate answered quickly, not sure that she would feel comfortable sitting with Sebastian in her new, very trim swimsuit. 'I wonder what we've got?' she thought aloud, pangs of hunger beginning to gnaw at her. Jasmine had packed a substantial meal: spicy hot chicken drumsticks and delicately spiced rice studded with fat raisins and topped off with slivers of coconut. Here was a salad of tropical fruits: fresh mango with juicy pineapple and purple passion seeds. Several bottles of the local Tusker beer jostled against a home-made crusty loaf that had been wrapped up in a soft, freshly laundered white linen tablecloth. Kate's appetite was aroused by the cocktail of aromas; she suddenly felt very hungry indeed. She sank her teeth deeply into a piece of chicken and her eyes filled immediately with tears. She gasped, eating as quickly as she could to rid her mouth of the burning chilli sensation. She waved her hand in front of her face, blowing frantically as her cheeks burned. Sebastian looked up then sat up immediately, pulling a bottle of beer from the box and flipping off the top. He placed the cold rim of the beer bottle on Kate's soft lips, encouraging her to drink. She swallowed gratefully, almost choking as the cold fizzy liquid filled her mouth. She swallowed the icy fluid and gasped as her throat cooled.

'That was hot!' she exclaimed.

'Serves you right for being so greedy,' laughed Sebastian, taking a generous mouthful of beer and wiping his mouth with the back of his hand before offering the bottle back to Kate.

'I'd forgotten just how hot Jasmine's spicy chicken could be,' Kate confessed, taking a drink and passing the bottle back. 'Do you want some?' she asked, offering Sebastian the chicken. He eyed the box dubiously. 'Go on, it's delicious — hot but delicious.'

'All right,' he agreed, taking a piece while Kate pulled a hunk of bread from the loaf. For a time they both sat contentedly, eating the picnic in comfortable silence. The sun was high in the clear sky, the beach deserted; it was like paradise and the sun's rays were heating Kate more and more but she still refused to take off her shorts. She felt vulnerable enough in such close proximity to him without adding to the tension that teased at her every muscle. Sebastian ate heartily; the swim had obviously given him an appetite.

'You've a crumb there,' he said, pointing to the corner of her mouth. Kate stuck her tongue to it, flicking tentatively to remove the offending crumb of bread, but it refused to budge.

'Here, let me,' he said, his voice as warm as the sun that was heating her body. He lifted his hand, reaching out to touch her, stroking her chin with a gentle swoop of his well-manicured finger. She felt the rough pull of the bread as it fell away but Sebastian's fingers remained motionless and slowly he began to outline her lips with a fingertip. She moved back, tormented by his touch, the burning intensity of his gaze heating the blood within her. He studied her, her face tilted upwards and an angry confusion flickering in her troubled eyes.

'Katy.'

She turned away. What had happened to her armour? Her protective shield was her control over her so powerful emotions. She stared out to sea, envious of its tranquillity, when she was lost in a storm of emotions.

'Katy,' Sebastian repeated, the use of her childhood name acting like an incantation to evoke the past. Memories flooded into her mind. She had not realised how much she had missed this gentle familiarity, how much she had missed being called Katy. She remained still, apprehension and anticipation jostling for supremacy.

'I think it's time to go back,' she said tonelessly as she gathered the tablecloth corners and deposited everything into the picnic bag. Sebastian watched her actions in silence for a moment, then scrambled to his feet, dragging on his clothes. His actions were hurried and betrayed his deep-rooted anger. They began to walk back to the boat, a wall of resentment building between them that neither wanted to scale.

* * *

Kate pushed away the fine mosquito net that draped her bed and moved towards the window. The night was still, disturbed only by the call of some far-away nocturnal bird. She opened the window a little wider, allowing a cool draught of air into her room. She couldn't sleep, tired though she was from the exertions of the day. Her mind was still too active. She replayed each moment with the same crystal-clear clarity. She could see his expression, the movements of his body, feel the warmness of his touch as his hand stroked the corner of her mouth.

She sighed, then took a deep breath, inhaling the fresh, sweet air delicately fragranced by the abundance of flowers that filled the garden. She looked up into the heavens and saw the sky sprinkled with millions of starlights. She mentally called on the gods to help her. She couldn't go on like this, being so close to him and knowing that he cared so little. And yet had she not seen that he did? Not felt?

She shook her head; brother and sister, old friends, that was how he saw them. It was her own foolishness that made her think otherwise. She interpreted his reactions as expressions of love but they weren't and it hurt—the situation was impossible.

'Damn him,' she cursed to the solitary moon before climbing back into bed and staring at the ceiling, unable to settle. Finally she fell into a fitful sleep but she awoke determined to resolve the situation. She wasn't prepared to take any chances. Yesterday's incident with Sebastian had only confirmed her worst fears. Still, despite her logical mind telling her that she was foolish, she wanted him. She knew she only had one alternative—to keep well out of his way. That morning she was determined to go to town, anything to avoid Sebastian.

'On you own?' echoed Clare when Kate announced that she was going. 'Are you sure you'll be all right?' she asked, pouring Kate's coffee with a doubtful look on her face.

'Yes, of course, I'll be fine,' laughed Kate, avoiding the look that Sebastian was giving her, his disapproval apparent without his even uttering a word. She shifted uncomfortably in her chair as she helped herself to some freshly baked bread, still warm from the oven. 'It's market day, I thought it would be fun,' she said, helping herself to the thick juicy marmalade that glowed invitingly in a cut-glass dish.

'It will be hot and overcrowded,' Sebastian stated.

'I thought I'd go and see if I could pick up any bargains,' Kate continued, effectively cutting out Sebastian by directing her conversation solely at her parents, though she knew he was listening to every word. 'I glimpsed some marvellous carvings on the way here. I just have to take one back. One of those warriors would look fantastic in my flat,' she explained, disregarding the snort of amusement from Sebastian.

'Well, just remember your luggage allowance.' Her father grinned affectionately, already withdrawing his wallet from the inside pocket of his jacket.

'No!' protested Kate, recognising the familiar pattern and no longer needing money as a sign of love. 'Honestly, I've plenty of my own money; besides, I shan't be buying anything that expensive.'

For a moment her father looked disappointed, but then he pushed his wallet back into his jacket and raised his eyebrows to Sebastian, who had watched the exchange with interest.

'These independent women!' Howard scoffed in mock-horror. 'Well, at least let Sebastian take you up to town—he has some business there and he can pick you up later.'

Kate's eyes darted in alarm to Sebastian; that was the last thing she wanted. She was trying to avoid him, not spend time with him. 'I'm not going just yet,' she lied, stalling for time and knowing that Sebastian would want to leave directly after breakfast.

'I'll wait,' he said grimly, his eyes flashing a warning to Kate that actually he would not want to be kept waiting too long. Kate swallowed at the dry lump forming in her throat and took a large mouthful of coffee to help ease the tightness. She knew she had no alternative but to agree to the arrangements. She finished her breakfast and picked up her bag, eager to be off to spend a day on her own.

'I'm ready,' she told Sebastian as she slipped her arms into a lightweight long cardigan that she could easily slip off and into her bag later when the sun grew too hot.

The drive into the town passed quickly, much to Kate's relief, and the bustling crowds made a colourful picture that she longed to be part of.

'I'll pick you up at twelve-thirty outside that bar. Be there!' Sebastian warned, thrusting the car into gear and roaring off, leaving Kate choking on the warm red dust that his car wheels had disturbed.

She began to investigate various stalls. Each one specialised in a particular trade. Some displayed small leather items: gloves, belts, purses. Others had larger leather garments: waistcoats with ornate tooling scrolled into the sides, or large leather holdalls. Wood carvings ranged from miniature pieces to huge designs, standing at least three feet tall, but it was the silks that really caught Kate's attention. The vast array of designs and colours was amazing, as if someone had captured a rainbow. A woman greeted Kate with a huge welcoming smile, unravelling her fabrics with a flourish and offering to make Kate any item of clothing she cared to name. It was impossible to resist; within moments, Kate was being measured up. She ordered a beautiful teal-blue stone-washed silk, with a very fine silver thread running throughout it, for a fraction of what it would have cost back in England. She also ordered a pair of loose trousers, and a camisole top with a matching long blouse. It was a perfect three-piece for the evening. She then wandered happily from stall to stall, buying an intricate carved figure, a colourful woven shoulder-bag, and before long she was weighed down with the amount she had bought. The sun was growing hotter and her arms ached with the strain of carrying so much. She knew her cheeks were pink and she pushed her fringe back off her damp forehead as she tried to push her way through the heaving crowds which now seemed to press down upon her, making moving difficult. Her feet ached, her head was beginning to throb and her English manners were getting her nowhere: nobody seemed to be able to hear her polite requests over the hustle and bustle.

'Excuse me, excuse me,' she said breathlessly, cursing herself for buying so much as her bags thumped against her sore legs. One of the bag straps suddenly gave way and Kate was near to tears as the contents emptied themselves on to the ground.

'A damsel in distress,' a heavy-accented voice crooned at her as a tall man dropped to his haunches and began to retrieve her packages.

'A knight in shining armour, I hope,' replied a grinning Kate, glad of some help, and immediately responding to the kind stranger who had come to her rescue.

'Here. Allow me,' he drawled, relieving Kate of her bags and collecting her parcels together. 'Would you like a drink?' he asked, inclining his head to indicate one of the roadside bars. 'You look like you need one.'

'Love one,' agreed Kate. It was just what she needed. She sank exhausted into a rickety wicker chair, under the cooling whirl of an electric fan.

'Mmm, what's this?' she asked as she tasted the deliciously sweet drink, her tongue quite unconsciously flicking over her softly parted lips.

'Mango and lemonade—it's delicious, yes?'

'Yes, wonderful,' agreed Kate, looking up and realising for the first time just how handsome her companion was. He had steel-grey eyes, sharp and intelligent, straw-coloured hair, cut in a precise shape, and a face that looked as if it had been carved from an excellent piece of perfect marble. Yet his features were softened by his full, sensuous mouth.

'My name is Allan—Allan Doran,' he said, extending his hand, unembarrassed by the scrutiny that Kate was subjecting him to. It was obvious that he was a man used to admiring looks from women.

'Kate—Kate Peterson,' she replied, enjoying the

warm strength of his hand as it enveloped hers. His thumb rubbed over her wrist, sending a tingle of anticipation the length of her arm.

'You are here on holiday?' he asked, looking at the assortment of parcels around Kate's feet.

'Yes, sort of. . .' Kate hesitated. 'A family reunion really. And you?' she asked, not wanting to dwell on her personal problems—and Allan was an excellent distraction.

'Business, unfortunately,' he said, drawing his mouth down in a sulky look that made Kate giggle. Sebastian always wore clothes to suit the climate and this man looked strangely out of place, still wearing a smart western suit in the heat. Kate couldn't help but compare his dress with Sebastian's more casual look.

'Business?' she asked, tipping the rest of her drink into her mouth. He looked far too slick to be engaged in business in Africa.

'Another?' he said, already turning his head to attract the young boy's attention with an assuredness that was rather attractive.

'Please.'

'Would you like a bite to eat to go with it?'

Kate remained silent for a moment, but the warmth of the sun, the easy conversation and her desire to forget Sebastian outweighed any doubts. Still, she couldn't help but wish she were sitting with Sebastian. She tended to compare all men to him, and not one of them came even close to the mark—not even Allan.

'It is lunchtime.' He glanced at the wafer-thin expensive gold watch that gleamed against his bronze skin. 'And I do hate to eat alone,' he added persuasively.

'It will be my pleasure,' said Kate with a smile.

'And mine,' he said smoothly, his voice smoky and his eyes dancing with delight. 'Let's go to the beach. I know a wonderful place.' He was already on his feet and collecting up Kate's parcels.

The restaurant on the beach was wonderful. It was situated in a low building of pure white, and had a large veranda reaching out on to the silvery beach. The aromas from a long black range barbecue, set up on the sand, filled the air.

'Please sit down.' Allan drew out a chair with a flourish and Kate sat down, enjoying the expensive surroundings. The wooden veranda afforded them a wonderful view of the beach and also protection from the heat of the midday sun. The colour scheme of apple-green and soft candy-pink gave an air of sophistication to the white cane furniture. The glassware was fine and delicate, decorated with a thin gold rim, and an artistic display of native flowers adorned the table.

'It's lovely here,' Kate gasped, unable to suppress her pleasure. 'The menu is wonderful too,' she said, carefully focusing on the lists to avoid the interest which she saw flickering in the depths of Allan's eyes. It pleased and alarmed her. He was charming, but a little too charming. He was not like Sebastian—he had an easygoing charm. Allan's was a little too polished and she felt he used it deliberately to attract women rather than it being a natural asset.

'How about something off the barbecue?' he asked, pointing to a young local man who was holding up a huge freshly caught fish that was speared and waiting to be cooked.

'Amazing,' Kate said as she saw the size of the fish

and admired the rainbow of colours that gleamed on its wet skin.

'Let's have lobster. Yes?'

'Sounds great.'

'Do you want wine?' Allan asked, pulling his chair a little closer and leaning forward. Kate felt threatened by his actions but put her worry down to a culture difference. Though she couldn't place where he was from, he definitely wasn't English. She shook her head, her fringe swishing to and fro, drawing attention to her eyes.

'No, it's a little early for me.'

'Good. I have a meeting later and I like to keep a clear head.'

For some reason, Kate didn't know why, she felt a sense of relief when he told her he would not be drinking. When she thought about it, there was something about him she didn't trust. The food arrived at once and Kate wasted no time breaking open the shining orange shell of the lobster and squeezing sharp lemon juice over the pure white flesh.

'This is what I call fast food,' she laughed, enjoying the lobster's faint smoky flavour. Allan joined in her laughter and Kate's heart soared. She felt appreciated for once.

'What line of business are you in?' she asked as she tucked into her food with obvious relish.

'At the moment I'm trying to prevent someone starting a business.' Allan smiled, but his voice held a grim note.

'Why?' she asked, intrigued by his secretive reply.

His expression grew serious and he leaned over the table, his steel-grey eyes fixed firmly on her.

'This company, the Duplas Co-operative, will be exploiting the people, paying low wages, ensuring huge profits,' he told Kate. But he had no need to explain: her own work for the Third World charity had given her an insight into the problems of a country such as this. She frowned, unable to place the name from her work, but knew she had heard the name Duplas just recently. A frown marred her forehead as she struggled to remember where. Allan stroked his strong fingers over her forehead, massaging her wrinkles away.

'Ah, that's better,' he crooned as Kate blushed. 'How delightful; I had no idea ladies still blushed.' Kate grew even more crimson and lowered her head. Allan pressed his fingers under her chin, forcing her to raise it again. A smile broke gently across Kate's face that was mirrored in Allan's. For a moment they were lost in each other's eyes, till a sharp voice cut the atmosphere between them.

'Kate! Here you are!' Sebastian bit out, casting a brief look at Allan which spoke of his disapproval. Kate suffocated her natural desire to argue with Sebastian and instead introduced the two men.

'Sebastian, this is Allan,' she said, explaining their relationship. Allan's eyebrows rose for a second in interest.

'I'm sorry to intrude,' Sebastian said, his sincerity lost in the dour expression on his face, 'but I think it's best if we return home.'

Kate got to her feet immediately.

'Why, what's happened?' There was a trace of hysteria in her voice that Allan responded to. He was at her side immediately.

'Your father is not well,' Sebastian said gravely.

'What do you mean?' Kate was now anxious and afraid.

'I think it's a mild angina attack. We'd best get back.'

'I had no idea. . .' she began hurriedly, already scrambling to pick up her parcels.

'I'm sorry our meal has come to such an abrupt end,' said Allan, flashing Kate a brilliant smile. 'I hope your father will be all right.'

'Yes, yes,' agreed Kate. 'I'm sorry but I must go; he hasn't been well, you see,' she explained as she began to follow Sebastian. 'Thanks for lunch,' she called over her shoulder as Sebastian grabbed her arm and pulled her.

'Another time, perhaps?' answered Allan, but Kate had no time to reply.

'Get your hands off me,' she threw at Sebastian.

'With pleasure,' he snarled. 'The car is over there.' He pointed to his car, which was already covered in a fine layer of red dust. Kate strode over, her anger apparent in her short, swift strides. In her hurry she dropped one of her parcels. Sebastian moved quickly to retrieve it, but not fast enough, and Kate snatched it from him.

'A real gentleman would be carrying these,' she scoffed, casting a look of disgust at him and ignoring the fury that burned in his eyes.

'Someone like Allan?' he came back, his body stiff with indignation.

'Yes, that's right. Someone like Allan,' she retorted briskly, mentally comparing the two different attitudes. Yet she knew whose company she preferred.

'Huh! Some gentleman,' huffed Sebastian, 'picking up young girls.'

'He did not pick me up,' cried Kate outraged by his accusation.

'No?' he mocked. She felt a crimson glow cover her cheeks and she pulled open the car door, throwing her packages into the back.

'No! He did not pick me up and I'm not a young girl but a full-grown woman,' she retorted, glaring at Sebastian as she climbed into the car and slammed the door. He ignored her completely as he got into the driver's seat, swung the car in a full circle and began to drive out of the town.

'Fully grown woman!' He laughed cruelly. 'You're a silly spoilt child who thinks of no one but herself.'

'How dare you. . .?' Kate began, furious at his attitude, though her chin quivered as she turned her face to confront him and was surprised by the look of regret in his eyes.

'I dare all right, Kate, and I tell you why: I know you. I know you better than you know yourself. I knew you would tire of playing nurses and want to spice up your life again and I didn't have to wait long, did I?' he growled, sparing her none of his temper.

Hot bitter tears burned at the back of Kate's eyes, but she blinked them quickly away, exchanging her hurt for anger.

'I have been taking care of my father, not playing nurses,' she protested.

'You're just so selfish, aren't you? Running off at the first opportunity—leaving it all up to my mother,' he flared.

Kate frowned at the mention of Clare. She had

helped her so much, but it was very difficult. The atmosphere between them was so strained as they both tried to please Howard.

'You're not being fair,' she replied.

'Not being fair? What would you know about that? All you ever think about is yourself. What about Clare, your father?' Sebastian asked, his wafer-thin control on his temper fading.

'I do care. . .'

'Well, you have a funny way of showing it,' he snapped.

'How is he, Sebastian?' she asked, her voice quieter now as the truth began to dawn on her.

'I don't know. Let's get back and find out,' he growled. 'I've wasted enough time looking for you.'

'You didn't have to,' she retorted, knowing she was grateful that he had, but he always seemed to bring out the worst in her.

'I wish to God I didn't, but unfortunately, you tiresome child, I was forced to yet again,' Sebastian said with slow deliberation.

'How noble. . .' started Kate, her voice thick with sarcasm.

'Don't push it, Kate. I've really had quite enough,' he warned. His face had drained of all colour; he was white with rage but Kate was indifferent to his emotions; she was too involved with her own. She had to stand up to him, make him realise that she was no longer a child.

'*You've* had enough. . .' she echoed his words in disbelief. 'You were downright rude to Allan.'

'Don't worry. I can assure you he's not the sensitive type.'

'How would you know?' said Kate, hating the superior ring to Sebastian's voice.

'I had to ask to find out where you were and some local lads knew exactly who you had gone with and where,' he replied, forcing the car into a higher gear and pressing down hard on the accelerator.

'Allan is a well-respected businessman who tries to help the local community,' Kate defended.

'Sure.'

Kate ignored the sarcastic ring to his reply and merely said, 'I thought he was quite attractive.' Sebastian said nothing, so Kate prompted, 'Didn't you?'

'He's not my type,' he joked drily. 'I prefer females.'

'Well, he is attractive,' Kate protested, casting a covert glance at Sebastian.

'Kate, I'm not interested,' he bit out through clenched teeth, his jaw so tight that it looked rock-solid.

'In what?' asked Kate innocently, her eyes wide and a soft smile curling her mouth.

'In playing games,' he bit out, not taking his eyes from the road.

'Games?' she said, enjoying the look on his face.

'I'm not jealous. Get it?' he growled, slamming on the brakes, stopping the car and turning to Kate. 'I've never cared about you in that way—to me you're just a kid, and a spoilt one at that,' he told her, before turning his attention back to starting the car up again and driving off.

Kate felt as if she had been struck, yet she only had herself to blame. She had tried to push him into admitting emotions he did not feel and now all she was left with was a sense of aching loss.

CHAPTER EIGHT

THE drive back was conducted in uncomfortable silence. Kate stared hard out of the window, feeling hurt and stupid. She had thought she had rid her system of all feelings for Sebastian; instead they remained as strong as ever. She longed to be far away from him, back in her tiny flat, alone but sheltered from the pain she was feeling now. Sebastian would only ever see her as a silly little girl, that was obvious, and Kate knew the only way to survive the rest of the time here was to steer well clear. That hadn't worked so far, she was forced to admit ruefully, not understanding why her stepmother had been so insistent that Sebastian drive her into town. She would have been perfectly safe.

'I'll bring your packages in,' he growled as he brought the car to an abrupt halt outside the house. 'You'd better go straight in, let them know you're back,' he added as he began to scoop Kate's purchases off the back seat.

'Thanks,' mumbled Kate, scurrying from the car; the sooner she was away from him the better. Her quick steps faltered as she saw Louisa in the doorway.

'Come along, Kate,' Louisa scolded like a senior prefect at Kate's old school. 'Your father wouldn't go up for his nap till you returned and he really is tired, you know.' The reprimand in her voice annoyed Kate, but she smiled sweetly in response, even disguising her anger when she heard Louisa say to Sebastian, 'Have you ever known such inconsiderateness?'

Kate went outside to the little patio where her parents were sitting in the shade of the dark-leaved trees that formed a cool canopy overhead.

'I'm back,' she said softly, then paused as she looked at her father. He didn't look at all well. His eyes looked heavy and his face was ashen. 'Daddy!' she cried in distress, dropping to his side. 'How are you? What happened?' she asked, a cold, clammy dread coming over her.

'A little tired, that's all. Clare tends to panic,' he said, with a weak smile. 'I'll go and have my rest now you're back,' he added, patting her arm affectionately.

'Yes, yes, do. I'm sorry I was late. I just got carried away,' Kate began to explain hurriedly, hating to see the distress she had caused. She glanced up at Clare, her eyes pleading, and Clare nodded in quiet under-standing, though Sebastian was still in bad humour.

'Buying this rubbish,' he said grimly as he scornfully deposited the parcels on to the floor.

They fell in disarray and Kate scrambled over immediately, protesting strongly, 'They're not rubbish! The pieces I chose were all made by craftsmen. See——' She held up a tiny, exquisitely carved elephant complete with two tiny tusks.

'Wonderful,' commented Sebastian drily, but a flicker of interest stirred in his face.

'Yes, it is.'

'I hope those tusks aren't real ivory,' he said, taking the elephant from Kate's hand and examining it closely.

'No—at least I don't think so,' she said doubtfully.

Sebastian tutted. 'Really, Kate, one should only buy anything ivory from the officially designated shops. At least then you know the ivory hasn't been poached. It's OK; this isn't ivory anyway,' he added, seeing her crestfallen face as he passed her tiny elephant back.

'I'd love to see some real ones,' said Kate wistfully, stroking the elephant's tusks.

'Would you?' asked her father, suddenly sounding brighter and looking animated.

'Yes, wouldn't you? It must be fascinating to see the animals in their natural habitat.'

Howard Peterson just smiled at his daughter's enthusiasm. 'Well, I'm off for a rest. I feel a bit tired. I'll be down for dinner,' he reassured Kate, rubbing his hand over the top of her head, and she raised her eyes to look at him, seeing him for once as a fragile old man. She was on her feet in seconds, putting her arms around him and hugging him tightly. 'I love you,' she whispered in his ear as she released him.

Sebastian watched silently, a frown creasing his brow. He raked his hair away from his face in a gesture of frustration. His action caught Kate's attention and she looked at him, his expression holding a deep stillness that made her wonder what he was thinking and why he was staring at her so intently. His eyes stayed on her for a moment, taking in the gentle look of love on her face, the soft parting of her lips as she smiled at her father, then he turned away, almost hurrying from the room. Kate sighed—was it always to be this way between them? A constant battle, a long fight that there seemed no respite from? She carefully gathered up her parcels and made her way to her room.

It was too hot to do anything and the sight of her freshly made bed, the crisp white cotton sheets already turned down, was all the invitation Kate needed. She took off her clothes and slipped naked into bed, enjoying the feel of the cold sheets against her heated body. It was a couple of hours later before she awoke and she certainly felt refreshed. She glanced at her watch and as there was plenty of time before dinner she decided on a long, leisurely bath.

She dressed with special care that night—she wanted to look different, more sophisticated than the girl they all saw her as. She flipped though her new wardrobe and chose a simple grey dress. It had a wide scooped neck of intricate lace offset by a tiny row of grey pearl buttons that ran down the fitted top, before it flowed into a full skirt. Kate twirled round, admiring herself in the mirror; the slim strappy sandals she wore added to the overall effect and she decided to wear her hair up. She carefully brushed it to one side before clipping it into a French pleat, revealing her long, slender neck. A pair of her mother's antique pearl drop earrings added to the complete picture of a sophisticated woman. She applied a shadow of colour across her lids, a mere brush of mascara and a quick spray of her most adult perfume.

'I'm crazy,' she murmured, her lips curling into a smile, yet for once she knew she wasn't doing this for Sebastian's benefit but for herself. She allowed herself to pause for effect at the lounge door before entering, her glance drifting over everyone till they became aware of her presence. Clare was the first to react with a mixture of surprise and delight.

'Kate!' she gasped, rising to her feet and drawing

her daughter into the room, her eyes shining with pleasure. 'I can't believe it's you. You look wonderful!'

Kate hesitated, then laughed at the back-handed compliment, casting a quick look around the room and taking in the admiring glances. Almost unconsciously her eyes sought out Sebastian. He sat holding a small tumbler of amber-coloured liquid that Kate guessed was whisky—his favourite tipple before dinner. Louisa was sitting at his side, her body curved into his, her perfectly manicured hand resting on his knee and her fingers lightly tracing a circular pattern. He raised his brows, his eyes filled with laughter, and Kate's confidence toppled for a moment. But she swiftly recovered as a tray of champagne was put before her. She took a glass, allowing the crystal rim to reach her lips before letting a smile curve her soft mouth. It was then that she caught the blaze of hostility from Louisa—a look of pure hatred—though Kate was unaware of any crime she had committed. She shuddered as Louisa's eyes narrowed on her with a fiery intensity that was almost threatening.

She turned away from them both. They were well-suited, she thought grimly, trying to ignore the dull ache that seeing them together evoked in her. Louisa looked stunning: the dress she was wearing fitted like a second silken skin, snugly fitting around every curve. Kate could never hope to compete against such sophistication and she immediately felt gauche.

Clare introduced Kate to the gathered guests, a collection of English people, all of whom had either permanent or holiday homes in the area. Conversation flowed easily, nothing too taxing—everyone was far too relaxed and in holiday mood to think about the world's problems—and Kate suddenly realised how much she was enjoying herself. She had often been invited out with people from work but they were somehow reserved affairs—everyone too conscious of their work, thus preventing them from really relaxing. Kate deftly avoided Sebastian all night, side-stepping him, or leaving a circle of people just as he approached. He had made no comment on how she looked and Kate's hope faded with every passing moment. When dinner was served she quickly attached herself to a Mr Dennison, a retired civil servant, who seemed only too delighted with her company.

It was a delicious meal. Clare enjoyed cooking and had been on several cordon-bleu courses. She loved entertaining and using local ingredients in new and exciting ways. Everyone complimented her on the delicate flavours and the subtle taste of spice that bit gently at the palate. Kate found herself sitting opposite Sebastian and she tucked her legs firmly under her chair so that there could not be the least chance for him to tease her. It was a game they had often played, giving each other quick kicks when something or someone amused them at dinner.

'Your legs will ache,' he suddenly said to her in a hushed tone. She tried to dimiss his observation but he continued, 'I can't feel your feet at all—where are they?' He shuffled his feet under the table.

'We're a bit too old for games like that, aren't we?' she hissed back, suddenly wondering if anyone had heard him, as it would seem a very odd conversation. She kept her expression and voice indifferent to him and turned her attention to her partner.

'Kate,' Sebastian persisted, and she swung back,

irritated by his constant interruptions, especially when it meant she had to suffer the glacial looks that Louisa was directing at her.

'Yes,' she snapped.

'Enjoying yourself?' he grinned, knowing that she was finding the evening a strain. Kate gave a slight nod in acknowledgement, a serene smile touching the corners of her mouth.

'Yes, thank you,' she said curtly.

'Yes, you look wonderful, Kate,' Louisa said, leaning forward, determined to be included. Her voice was warm but there was more than a trace of coolness in her guarded expression. 'You must be very proud of your *little* sister,' she said, emphasising the word 'little' as she turned to Sebastian. Her expression suddenly changed and her eyes became soft and suductive, her voice deeper and husky, and her face smoothed of all the hard sharpness that she seemed to reserve for Kate exclusively.

Sebastian's mouth slanted in a warm and lazy smile. 'She looks like a painted doll,' he said, looking back at Kate whose lips curved in automatic response, effectively hiding the pain of his remark, in direct contrast to the way Louisa's were thinning to a tight line at the banter, her eyes diamond-hard as she looked at Kate.

'Howard!' The piercing scream of Clare tore between them and they both reacted at once. Howard Peterson was clutching his chest, his hands in tight fists as he doubled over. His face was drained of all colour and his lips had taken on a disturbing blue outline.

'Phone for the doctor!' Sebastian barked. 'And please clear the room,' he ordered the guests, who seemed trapped by some macabre fascination and were watching the proceedings with a morbid curiosity.

'Open your mouth, put this under your tongue,' Kate said in a firm but quiet voice, gently pushing a tiny white tablet into her father's mouth. 'You'll be all right; just relax,' she said soothingly, casting an anxious glance at Clare who stood nonplussed at his side, too shocked to move. Kate's fingers entwined around her father's wrist carefully, feeling for his pulse: it felt weak and erratic.

'Could you carry him?' she asked Sebastian.

'I'll manage,' he replied briefly.

'No,' Howard croaked, and there was a determination in his voice that caused Sebastian to pause. 'Just give me a minute or two; it's already easing off,' he told them in short, gasping breaths.

'He's right,' agreed Clare, her husband's voice breaking through her shock. 'Just help me get him to our room. I'll see to him.' She gave Kate an affectionate smile. 'He'll be OK. He's just done too much,' she reassured her, grateful for the help. Kate's eyes fastened on Clare's and for once they were together, emotionally linked in their love for one man. In that moment an understanding sprang between them, and when Clare smiled at her Kate smiled glowingly back.

Kate sat on the patio, the blackness of the night suiting her mood. She stared with vacant eyes into the darkness, her whole body numb except for the dull pain in her own chest. The doctor was still with her father and she had left Sebastian to see to the guests; she couldn't face them now. She wanted to be alone. She knew she couldn't face the polite enquiries after her father's health or the sympathetic and pitying looks she was bound to receive. All she wanted was to be alone, to try and find some peace and tranquillity amid all the turmoil.

'Kate?'

She didn't answer. Her mouth was dry and she couldn't bear to hear any bad news. She wanted to shut it out. She knew it was her fault. She had seen the state he was in when she had come back late from her shopping expedition. It had all been too much— the worry, the lack of rest. It was all her fault and she couldn't bear it, the look of accusation in Sebastian's eyes.

'Kate, Kate, he's all right. He's going to be all right.' Sebastian's words hung in the cool night air before slowly sinking into Kate's consciousness. 'Kate, did you hear?' he persisted, joining her outside and shivering as he realised how much the temperature had dropped. He sat down beside her and and gave a gasp of surprise.

'You'd best come in, Kate.' His voice was soft but firm. 'Come on,' he coaxed, gently wrapping his arm around her shoulders and drawing her back into the lounge. Idly, Kate looked up at the sky, covered with millions of stars.

'Just look at all those stars,' she said, her eyes skimming over the velvet heavens till Sebastian moved her.

'They're beautiful, Kate, just beautiful,' he murmured in her ear as he steered her back inside and sat her down. She was shivering slightly too, and he took off his jacket, placing it gently around her shoulders.

Then he slipped back and closed the patio doors. Kate sat staring into the flames of the mock-fire, the pain of guilt weighing heavily on her.

'Here, drink this,' Sebastian commanded, pushing a glass of brandy into her hands. 'He's all right, Kate; it was just an angina attack. He's going to have to take things a bit more easy, that's all.'

'I know.' She sounded slightly breathless, her voice hollow.

'Then what is it, Kate? What's wrong?' Sebastian asked, obviously troubled by her blank expression. Kate leapt to her feet, Sebastian's jacket falling into a crumpled heap at her feet.

'I've got to go,' she said quickly, her voice filled with panic. 'Now. I've got to go now,' she added breathlessly, her eyes darting around the room while she looked for a means of escape.

'Go? Go where?' demanded Sebastian, getting to his feet, troubled by her behaviour.

'I can't stay,' she said. 'You see that?' she asked, a desperate plea in her voice and her eyes searching his face for confirmation. 'I should never have come back, never!' she cried.

Sebastian took her firmly by the shoulders. He could hear the hysterical note that was entering her tone and had to prevent it getting any worse. He held her firmly.

'Kate?' he questioned softly, as he sought the source of the pain that troubled her so much.

'It's my fault, Sebastian, my fault,' she choked, the well of tears that she had fought so hard to control breaking into a flood until she was sobbing uncontrollably. 'You're right. I'm selfish and spoilt and I haven't changed a bit,' she spluttered.

Sebastian drew her to his chest, his arms enveloping her, and he rocked her to and fro. 'I've made him ill,' she said.

'Stop it, Kate, stop it!' he ordered. 'It's not your fault and nobody thinks it is,' he reassured her. Kate struggled to break loose from his arms, but he continued to hold her close while he explained, 'You know your father is a workaholic and he's still pushing himself too hard. He's supposed to be recuperating. He insists on still working and maybe this will show him he can't do that any more, so you can just stop blaming yourself right now.'

'I still shouldn't have come back,' she confessed quietly, half to herself. This felt too good, resting on Sebastian's chest, listening to the steady thud of his heart, feeling the warmth of him.

'Yes, you should,' he assured her, the familiar touch of his arm on her back making her feel slightly dizzy. 'I'm glad you're here,' he said softly, his warm breath touching her hair like a summer breeze.

'You are?' she asked, surprised by this admission. 'But you forced me here, made sure I came,' she said, doubting his sincerity.

'I had to. I had missed you so much, Kate.'

'Did you?'

'Yes, I did, but when the detective found you and I knew you were no longer a little girl but a woman with a life of her own to lead I decided to be a little heavy-handed,' he admitted sheepishly. 'You look wonderful tonight—quite grown-up. I hardly recognised you.'

'Do I?' In that brief moment Kate thought her heart would burst with joy.

'Stop fishing for compliments,' he joked.

'I'm not,' she protested weakly.

'Aren't you?'

'A little,' Kate agreed, sinking on to the couch beside him. 'I wanted to come back if I could have been assured of a welcome.'

'But you've always been welcome,' he began to protest, brushing a tendril of hair from her face. It was a feather-light touch but Kate could feel her resistance melting.

'Well, that puts an end to that idea,' Clare interrupted them. She was too preoccupied at first to notice the intimacy between the couple but when she did she just smiled.

'What idea?' Sebastian and Kate chorused in union.

'The safari. I've told him it's out of the question and the doctor agrees, so I'm afraid you'll have to go alone,' she finished quickly, seeing the protests already forming on their lips.

'Safari? I can't believe it,' Kate said, delighted, her eyes wide; but underneath there was a real fear—did Clare blame her for her father's set-back, so that she was no longer welcome here?

'Yes, you can,' Clare said firmly, her voice not brooking any argument. 'I insist. It was your father's wish—a little treat. He arranged it as a surprise. He'd feel awful if you didn't go—as if it was all his fault,' she explained calmly to Kate before fixing her attention on Sebastian. 'Now you can stop shaking your head. You can't expect Kate to go alone and unchaperoned. It can be dangerous so you'll have to go too.'

'Are you sure, Clare?' asked Kate. She hated the thought of leaving her to nurse her father alone. He was not an easy patient and could be quite argumentative.

'I'm quite sure, Kate.' Clare gave a knowing smile that Kate immediately picked up on—she wanted to be alone with Howard.

'I can hardly wait. I've always wanted to go.' She was hardly able to keep the glee from her voice.

'And you always get what you want, don't you?' said Sebastian quietly.

'It will be wonderful,' said Kate, ignoring Sebastian. She was doing this for Clare and Howard's sake and if he couldn't understand it she wasn't about to explain. Let him think the worst of her—he usually did.

Sebastian opened his mouth to protest but was cut off before he had the chance to start—his mother knew him too well. 'It's only for three days and it will do you both good,' she said firmly, putting an end to any further discussion. Kate turned and looked at Sebastian. He sent a challenging look her way, an ironic gleam in his dark eyes.

'Well, that's settled, then,' he said slowly, rising to his feet with a resigned air.

'You don't have to come with me,' Kate told him easily, suppressing a twinge of pain at his attitude, the pendulum swing of his mood. The intimacy they had just shared seemed completely forgotten.

'Not come with you?' he teased. 'I wouldn't miss it for the world.'

CHAPTER NINE

'*JAMBO, jambo,*' called the local driver, his eyes shining with natural friendliness. He reached out, pulling Kate on board an open-topped vehicle that afforded her a full view of the whole area. Sebastian climbed in beside her, a neat but obviously expensive camera slung over his broad shoulders. Kate caught the admiring glances he was receiving from the other passengers, both men and women alike. But she too was staring at him, drinking in the sight of his wide-open smile, the intelligent gleam in his eyes. Sebastian, used to the attention of others, was indifferent to them and slid into the chair next to Kate.

'Don't you look different!' she declared with unfeigned affection. 'I'm not surprised you're catching everyone's attention,' she teased.

'The Great White Hunter,' he agreed, with a ready smile and an ease Kate wished she could match. 'It's too hot for anything else,' he added by way of explanation, his hands dropping on to his bare thighs. Kate's gaze dropped briefly to his suntanned, firm thighs, fighting off the emotions he aroused within her, as she had done countless times before—never too successfully. This time she was determined that it would be different—had to be different, if they were to enjoy this trip.

'I'm looking forward to this,' Sebastian said to her, his smile deepening, causing small wrinkles to form

132

around his eyes. 'Give me a chance to use my new toy,' he said, tapping his camera with affection.

'You weren't originally,' Kate reminded him, her tone deliberately light-hearted and friendly.

'No, to be honest, I wasn't,' he agreed.

She studied his face as he spoke; he was being frank as usual, but she would have preferred a white lie. 'Is my company that bad?' she asked, tempering her hurt with a gentle grin that lifted the corners of her mouth. She tried to understand the flicker of emotion that crossed Sebastian's face.

'It's not that, Kate. . .' he mumbled, and she sensed his discomfiture. He toyed with his camera, avoiding her eyes.

'What, then?' Kate probed, more intrigued than troubled by his obvious reluctance. He shrugged his powerful shoulders, feigning an indifference that she instinctively knew he was not feeling.

'Oh, you know.' A frown pleated his brow, drawing his dark brows in even further over his eyes.

'Do I?' challenged Kate, holding her head at a saucy angle as she waited for him to explain.

'Don't you?' he tossed back. His head lifted suddenly and his eyes trapped hers, waiting for her denial, but Kate dropped her gaze, unable to negotiate the undercurrent that always ran between them, threatening to overwhelm her.

'How long will it be before we set off?' she enquired. She had learnt that the only way to survive was to keep the conversation light and impersonal.

'Five minutes.' His expression became faintly grim, as if he objected to her changing the subject. 'Have you got your binoculars handy? The camouflage technique of these wild animals makes spotting them virtually impossible,' he explained.

'I didn't know you'd been on safari before,' commented Kate, jealous because she had wanted them to experience it for the first time together. They had so many shared memories, each emblazoned on her mind and heart with the red-hot steel of desire. Sebastian had introduced her to so many different things. He was an integral part of her life and would be forever. No matter how hard she tried to keep a barrier between them, she knew that it was impossible.

'I haven't,' Sebastian said, making Kate's dark thoughts vanish by his brightness. 'I just watch a lot of nature programmes on TV.' He laughed good-naturedly. As he relaxed his features softened, and the usual tension ebbed from his face.

'We're off!' cried Kate suddenly in excitement as the engine was started and the Jeep jumped forward.

'You're not going to sing, are you?' asked Sebastian with a theatrically pained expression on his face and mock-desperation in his voice.

'Do you remember?' Kate murmured wistfully, a sudden vivid image of herself as a young girl flashing through her mind.

'How could I forget?' Sebastian declared, raising his brows to heaven as his smile widened still further, creating deep grooves down the sides of his handsome face.

'It was the year we went to France,' Kate said, responding to the lighter side of his nature.

'That's right,' he agreed, flashing her another quick smile to soften the blow of his next words. 'And you drove us all mad singing that silly song.'

'Happy days,' sighed Kate, shaking her head in regret of the passing years that had flown by, leaving her only fond recollections.

'Childhood is full of such innocence,' Sebastian remarked quietly, picking up on her changing mood and watching her closely.

'Then we grow up,' Kate returned, surprising herself with the sadness that was present in her tone.

'That's right,' Sebastian said, briskly trying to break the seriousness of the conversation. 'We all change and nothing ever stays the same.'

Kate half nodded in reply; she was thinking—thinking about the past and how she, and her life, had changed.

'I don't mind now,' she confessed, keeping her voice deliberately casual to avoid the confrontation that she knew might develop. She wanted to avoid that at all costs.

Sebastian looked down at the hand she had placed lightly on his bare arm, her long fingers soft against the coarse hairs on his skin.

'Mind what?' he asked, aware that she was serious, and he covered her hand with his.

Kate drew her hand away, startled by the wave of intensity that such a casual touch could produce. She looked at him, taking in the cool darkness of his gaze, the puzzled frown that creased his forehead. She felt a moment's hesitation, then she swept on, 'About the business. I don't think I would have been very good anyway,' she finished weakly, recalling the terrible scene she had caused and the pain and disruption that followed.

His glance flicked to her.

'I bet you would,' he answered her, surprising Kate by his sincerity. 'You always took such a keen interest,' he recalled with crystal-clear clarity, the admiration in his voice making her heart soar.

'Yes—yes, I did. But not because I was interested in engineering, but because I wanted to be part of the family company.' She tipped her head slightly back, her hair falling over her shoulders as she tried to gauge his reaction to this revelation.

'No?' he asked, partly intrigued, partly puzzled. 'But I thought. . .'

Kate shook her head gently from side to side, her action silencing him. 'No,' she began firmly. 'Daddy had been such a workaholic. I wanted his attention,' she confessed. 'Desperately,' she concluded.

'So you developed an interest in engineering?' Sebastian added, with an understanding nod, the interest in his eyes trapping her for a moment.

'It wasn't so much the partnership he offered you. . .' she mused absently, recalling the depth of emotion she had felt that day, the white-hot anger that had torn through her, the final straw that had pushed her to never wanting to see any of them ever again. Looking back, she had been a fool—a young girl fighting to come to terms with the turmoil of feeling that had swept through her as she had begun her struggle to maturity.

'You saw it as a rejection of you?' Sebastian probed gently. But he already knew the answer—he was too perceptive not to understand fully the implication of what he had just heard.

'That's right.' Her breathing had deepened and she tensed momentarily. 'I know I became impossible,' she said quickly, wanting to admit she was in the wrong and finding it difficult, though not as difficult as she would have thought.

'That's an understatement.'

Kate stole a glance at Sebastian's face, expecting condemnation, and her body sagged with relief.

'Well, I was determined to be noticed,' she defended herself, and she shifted uncomfortably in her chair.

'You certainly were,' Sebastian agreed, laughter bubbling up inside him, and the sound was totally infectious, so that Kate laughed too. 'Yet we expected you to come back despite the row,' he finished.

Kate grimaced as he spoke, furiously trying to think of a reply which would avoid telling Sebastian why she had not come home. 'I was homesick,' she finally admitted cautiously, 'especially for you.' I missed you more than anyone, she thought to herself as she looked at him.

'So, why didn't you come home?' he challenged. Kate froze; she heard his tone, the demand for a reply that she felt unable, unwilling, to give. She let the silence run on as she stuggled to choose the right words.

'I couldn't,' she said simply, her eyes dropping to her hands, which lay limply on her lap, her fingers twisting in agitation. 'I wasn't ready,' she added quietly.

'You still felt unwanted, rejected?'

He moved as he spoke, his actions and words flowing into one natural movement. He drew her towards him, allowing her head to sink on to his chest. Kate nodded, her head still bent, her eyes aching with the exertion of staring for so long and hard at her hands, unable to face him.

'Poor Katy,' he whispered as his fingers stroked her long hair, soothing and reassuring. 'I didn't realise. Perhaps I've misjudged you.'

Kate lifted her face to his. There was something in his expression that stirred old memories. Their closeness had rekindled the dangerous flame that flickered between them and Kate, frightened that she might be overwhelmed, swiftly sat up. She turned her head to look at the dusty red landscape, throwing Sebastian a glance that she hoped appeared casual, despite the vortex of emotions that now raged within her.

'Be careful, Sebastian'. She grinned playfully, the smile never reaching her troubled eyes. 'That sounds almost like an apology to me.'

She waited for him to speak but the clear voice of the guide cut in, his excited tone alerting everyone, and Kate was grateful for the distraction. She stared out across the landscape and narrowed her eyes, scanning the horizon, desperate to see the wildlife. It was difficult, because the animals blended into their habitat, but beyond the thorn bushes, amid the gauzy acacia trees that shimmered in the deep heat, Kate caught her first sight of the tall, long-legged giraffes. They seemed to drift in and out of the trees, their necks stretching to nibble at the very tops of the trees where the freshest, greenest leaves were. She gave a cry of delight as Sebastian trained his binoculars in order to achieve a clearer view. It was a breathtaking experience and they were warned to watch out for many more sightings.

White-bleached bones and barren carcasses were an indication that they were entering an area that was teeming with animals. The Jeep bounced over the bumps and ruts of uneven, dusty tracks. Kate continued to scan the landscape like a hawk as she tried to distinguish, in the hazy distance, animals from bushes and birds from branches. The sharp-eyed guides had no problem as they drove through the acres of the national park, instructing their audience where to look.

'No wonder most of the animals go under cover till dusk. This heat is exhausting me,' complained Kate, pulling a floppy hat from her bag and pushing it over her eyes to shelter her head from the relentless, hot sun rays.

'The heat and the fact that we set off at five-thirty. I didn't even know a time like that existed,' agreed Sebastian, his eyes now shielded by a pair of dark glasses.

'I feel sleepy,' murmured Kate, surprised at how close Sebastian was and forcing herself not to be affected by the nearness of him.

'Have a sleep, then, or you won't enjoy tonight,' he said softly. She could feel the warmth of him all the way down to her toes.

'Tonight?'

'Yes. Remember we have a grandstand view of the waterholes.'

Kate's mouth widened into a huge yawn and she nodded in agreement. 'You're right,' she said, settling down and resting her head on her elbow. The Jeep jolted over yet another rut in the uneven ground and her arm fell uncomfortably as she tried to settle.

'Come here,' Sebastian said tenderly, drawing her towards him again and resting her head on his chest. She couldn't look at him. 'Is that better?' he asked as she relaxed against him, responding immediately to his dangerous closeness.

Lifting her confused gaze to meet his, despite her resolve not to, she mumbled, 'Yes, fine thanks.'

His lips grazed across the top of her forehead.

'Then sleep.'

It was the gentlest command she had ever heard and obediently Kate allowed her head to fall heavily on his chest, enjoying the sound of his heart thumping against her ear. A thrill of forbidden desire stirred in the pit of her stomach, warning her that her safety-armour was not impenetrable. She closed her heavy-lidded eyes. She was much too tired to think about that now.

She fell asleep.

Nothing could have prepared her for the magnificent view that Sebastian awoke her to: the sun was already setting, turning the sky a vivid orange, bright and burning, that was a perfect backdrop for the bare ebony branches of the trees silhouetted against the flaming sky. The Shimba Hills rose like a row of uneven pyramids in the distance, shimmering behind a veil of heated mist that rose from the scorching earth.

'Come on, sleepyhead,' Sebastian said, offering Kate his hand as she climbed from the Jeep, her eyes still absorbing every inch of the vivid landscape, memorising every unique detail.

'Thanks for your shoulder,' she said, effectively covering her embarrassment as his hands wrapped around her waist and lifted her to the ground. 'I feel great now,' she reassured him, breaking loose from his grip then immediately sensing the loneliness she felt when his hands left her sides.

'You can have my shoulder any time.' Sebastian's tone was oddly wistful and strangely at odds with his usually efficient manner. 'See you at dinner in ten minutes.'

She knew she had to have a very quick shower and change, and her room turned out to be even more unusual and spectacular than she had expected. Better quarters were situated above ground in the tall, strong branches of an ebony tree. A veranda gave access to a splendid, never-ending view. Unfortunately, however, Kate had no time to waste on enjoying it. She knew Sebastian would not want to be kept waiting so she dived under the shower, amazed by the force of hot water that stung her tender flesh. Her hair was washed but she didn't have time to wait for it to dry. Instead she curled it carefully into a loose bun and secured it at the nape of her neck with an intricately carved wooden clasp. She slipped into a free-flowing coral silk skirt and topped it with a matching camisole with shoelace straps. Her face was beginning to tingle with the heat of the day's sun, which had taken its toll, so she did not bother applying make-up—just a thin layer of moisturiser.

She made her way carefully down the steps from her tree-house and over to the hotel restaurant. The rooms were all linked by a wooden bridge at a lower level that stretched from tree to tree. The restaurant was an impressive sight, the tables all strategically placed to allow everyone a full clear view of the waterhole. Kate paused, her eyes skimming over the other guests till they fell on Sebsatian. Her heartbeat quickened at the sight of him: he too had changed from his casual attire of linen shorts and shirt into a very formal dark suit. The whiteness of his shirt seemed brilliant against the dark cloth of his jacket and the subtle lighting of the restaurant. Kate watched him in the shadowy light, the glow of the candle softening the hard angles of his face yet not robbing it of the strong masculinity that was an integral part of his nature. He leaned back in his chair, his long legs outstretched and crossed casually at the ankle. He was gazing out into the night but his mind was clearly not on the view below. He was lost in private thoughts that Kate longed to share.

She took a deep breath, hoping to arm herself against him, as she marched across the room, a ready smile already forming on her soft mouth. His attention was caught before she reached him. There were few men who had not noticed her entrance—not that Kate was aware of them—she only ever had eyes for Sebastian.

'I bought you a beer,' he said as he drew out her chair, pausing slightly as he drank in the sight of her. 'You're looking good,' he added, the sincerity in his voice making her glow with pleasure. 'I thought you'd be thirsty.'

'Thank you, I am,' she said breathlessly, a little disturbed by the flicker of male interest that passed through his eyes. She slid into her chair, grateful that she could cover her own feelings by taking a drink. She poured her beer with a remarkably steady hand till a white frothy head edged the top of her glass, then raised the glass to her lips, aware that Sebastian's gaze was still on her with an interest she found unnerving.

She drank thirstily, finishing the tall glass without stopping. She grinned as she placed it back down on the table and caught Sebastian's stunned look.

'I needed that,' she gasped. 'I finished my bottle of water by mid-morning,' she offered by way of explanation.

'Come on, it's a buffet and I'm starved.' Sebastian rose with languid grace, his movements slow and deliberate, and he offered his outstretched hand to Kate. She hesitated. It was wrong, no man should be that damned attractive, she thought to herself, knowing that her lack of immunity to him was shared by most women. She tried to assume the relaxed air that came so naturally to him and stood to join him.

The buffet table cut the length of the restaurant, effectively making a barrier between the bar and the diners. The food was as colourful as an Impressionist's landscape, a vast array of bright, vivid colours splashed across a white linen tablecloth. It was hard to choose as each dish was a temptation: the spicy scents teased Kate's appetite still further and she went back to their table with an assortment of dishes.

'Here, try this,' Sebastian said with a wicked grin, leaning over the table and offering Kate a very orange tiger-bay prawn. She looked at it dubiously, casting a wary glance at Sebastian's face. His grin widened, and Kate's insides curled with delight as she opened her mouth like an innocent baby bird. She allowed her lips to close a little too soon and they touched Sebastian's fingers. She paused, her lips parting slightly to allow his escape, but her eyes were fixed on his, trapped in the smouldering depths of his dark gaze. She felt her pulse leap at the sudden atmosphere that seemed to have surrounded them. There was a disturbing quiet that was pregnant with a hidden undercurrent of sexual awareness. It was a dangerous game, but one that Kate longed to play.

'That's hot!' she complained, her throat burning with the spicy heat of the food, and she picked up Sebastian's glass, downing his beer to drown the burning sensation that permeated her mouth and stung her tender lips.

'Even hotter than Jasmine's chicken?' he asked, with a teasing grin, as he nodded to the waiter to bring a fresh supply of drinks.

'Even hotter,' admitted Kate, her eyes sparkling with delight as she cast her glance over her plate, looking for an equally tasty morsel.

'Have you any of this?' she teased, waving a twisted piece of chicken under Sebastian's nose in an attempt to entice him. She drew back as his mouth tried to snap the meat from her fingers, leaving him biting into air. He frowned and, with the sudden unexpected strike of a prowling animal, gripped her wrist, pulling her back over the table. She gave him a quick smile in defence but he paid no heed, despite her protests. His white teeth sank into the dark meat and he pulled his head back aggressively with a low growl.

'Mmm, delicious,' he crooned softly, his voice deepening with emotion and his grip relaxing to a slow caress over Kate's throbbing pulse. She froze; she couldn't play these games, flirting when she cared so much for him; it hurt far too much. She pulled her hand free, confused by his behaviour.

'Look at the waterhole,' she cried, glad of the distraction, and turned her chair round as a barrier against him as she forced herself to concentrate on the moving pictures outside.

'Lovely,' agreed Sebastian as a herd of cumbersome elephants with great grey ears waded in, sinking into the damp mud that surrounded the water, their trunks splashing before releasing a fountain of water into the sky.

Kate was silent. There was something in his smoky tone that warned her he was not referring to the animals but she did not risk contemplating what he did mean. She had been hurt before and was not prepared to leave herself open to that unnecessary pain again. She took another large mouthful of beer. It felt good— a gentle analgesic against what she felt. They talked, passing remarks about the wildlife, safe comments that Kate felt she could cope with. After a while it became dark but she continued to stare out into the safe dusk.

Suddenly, her reverie was interrupted by the steady beat of a drum. She jumped in surprise as a host of lights moved about in the darkness till the area below the restaurant was filled with a whole tribe of Masai warriors, their ochre wigs adding to their apparent ferocity. They stamped their feet as they drew closer, brandishing spears with a realism that startled Kate.

'It's all part of the holiday entertainment,' Sebastian reassured her, pulling her chair closer to his. She nodded, keeping her eyes fixed on the noisy display below. She took another mouthful of beer. It had been a long day and though the night air was chilly her skin still burned with the memory of the midday sun.

'What now?' she asked as the last warriors disappeared into the blackness of the night. She was growing more excited with every passing minute—this was the first time she had been in Sebastian's company and treated as an equal. She had begun to feel better and no longer threatened by the closeness of Sebastian, but delighting in his company. She was so thrilled—she wanted to enjoy each moment to the full.

'Dancing.'

'I love dancing,' she giggled, getting to her feet and pulling at the lapels on Sebastian's jacket. 'Come on, let's do it.'

Sebastian remained immobile, a troubled look on his face. He obviously did not want to dance with her. Despite how hard she had tried to make herself attractive, he never saw her that way. Kate suffocated her disappointment but nothing was going to dampen her spirits tonight. She did not wait for him to partner her, the music was far too infectious, the rhythm seemed to vibrate through her and she felt her feet joining the energetic beat with enthusiasm. She danced, twirling round and round, enjoying the incessant drum-beat that echoed through her head, shutting out her feelings for Sebastian as she became lost in the sway of bodies. Her laughter grew louder as she danced and she was unaware of the glitter of annoyance that gleamed in the depths of Sebastian's dark eyes. Every time he heard Kate laugh he flinched, as if struck by an unseen assailant. Finally he jumped to his feet. Kate was still dancing, her body swaying now in a slow, sensual movement that seemed to fuel Sebastian's temper. He marched across the floor, pressing firmly on the backs of the dancers who did not see his approach, though most did and moved swiftly.

'Come on, Kate,' he said, his voice as sharp and cutting as a newly sharpened knife.

But the music, combined with effects of the sun and the alcohol, was acting as a real confidence-booster to Kate and she objected to her fun being interrupted.

'Leave me alone,' she laughed. She shrugged off his grip and turned her body back towards the other dancers.

'Come and sit down.' Sebastian spoke through clenched teeth, his words coming out in a warning hiss that Kate paid no heed to.

'I don't want to sit down.' She swayed again to the music as she spoke, her hips moving sensuously. 'I'm enjoying myself, having a bit of fun.' She giggled and threw her arms around the man dancing next to her. Sebastian's body stiffened with anger, his face draining of all colour, his eyes freezing and hard.

'Kate!' he snapped, the quietness in his voice more effective than if he'd shouted. She paused and he caught her by the shoulders, twisting her round. 'Sit down now,' he commanded, a deep growl adding menace to his voice as he began to escort her firmly from the floor.

He pushed her into her chair. Kate picked up her glass of beer from the table—all the dancing had made her thirsty again—and began to drink, but Sebastian intervened. He took a firm grip on the glass, pulling it away from Kate with a flash of anger.

'I think you've had enough,' he told her, taking in the high flush on her cheeks with cold regard.

'I'm thirsty,' she protested, hating his high-handed attitude. Surely he couldn't imagine she was drunk on a couple of bottles of beer? But then, that was all he ever saw her as—a child—not the woman she had become. He had watched her grow, yet still, deep down, refused to acknowledge it.

'Then drink water,' he ordered, pulling her to her feet. She fell against him, her soft breasts hitting against the hard firmness of his muscular chest. The effect was both electric and sobering. She felt the heated flow of blood rush through her trembling body as she struggled to move away from the magnetic pull that seemed to draw them closer together.

'I think we'd better go up,' Sebastian told her. He drew her closer, his warm breath touching her skin and his familiar aftershave stirring hidden memories. She tensed for an instant, then smiled playfully and nodded in silent agreement.

'Where's your key, Kate?' he asked, with a flicker of exasperation, as she fumbled in her bag, still unsteady on her feet.

'Here.' She giggled as she waved the key in front of his eyes, enjoying the discomfort she was causing him, feeling sure it was because she was behaving exactly as he saw her: a silly child.

Sebastian snatched at the key, his patience finally coming to an end. He drew Kate close to him, his arm wrapping around her waist so that she was unable to escape.

'Come on,' he said abruptly, marching her out of the restaurant.

'Oh, aren't we masterful?' Kate crooned, twisting her fingers round his tie and pulling at it so that he was forced to lower his head. The brooding black look that welled in his eyes at her action alerted her to the thin control he had on his temper.

'Cut it out, Kate,' he growled, his features composed apart from the fine tension that pulled at the corners of his mouth.

'Why?' she said, being deliberately provocative but wanting to force the issue. She wanted him to see her as a woman, to admit to himself that he saw her as a mature adult—yet every time she seemed only to arouse his temper and not anything else. He closed his eyes to block her image out and shook his head. Kate dropped her gaze, saddened by his lack of response. She felt so foolish; all her attempts at seduction had failed miserably. She leaned against the door-jamb as Sebastian opened the door of her room. She flopped inside and he caught her arm to steady her as she kicked off her sandals.

She turned, her arm still trapped by his. The moon cast a shadowy light over the room, lighting it with a silvery sheen. She tried to smile at him, a smile of apology, but it slowly faded from her mouth as she saw there was no censure in his eyes, no trace of anger or disapproval. His eyes were bright and clear and the message that shone from them was unequivocal. She was trapped by that look, held by its intensity, and she knew in that moment that they were both lost in the heady sea of long-ago memories.

The moment seemed to stretch, lengthened by the silence that grew between them as the past seemed to rush up and threaten to overwhelm them. She stepped back, aware of the change between them and unable to comprehend it.

Her gaze shifted to his lips and seemed to fix there; the impulse to move towards him was irresistible. They moved in union, his lips descending lightly on hers.

Kate wanted to draw back the moment she felt his warm lips on hers but he did not allow her to move. His hand reached up, catching on the tight coil of hair that prevented him from cradling her neck. He pulled at her hair, releasing her tresses over her shoulders, the clip falling noisily to the floor.

Taken by surprise by the kiss, Kate's defences shattered as his warm lips became increasingly mobile, teasing away any last resistance. He was giving yet also demanding and Kate responded, luxuriating in the whirlpool of emotion he was so easily arousing in her. His hands were steady as he stroked her breast, awaking in her a flood of desire, her nipple growing tight as it pressed against her top. The thin silk provided little protection against his fingers as they explored the fullness of her breasts.

She held her breath as she trailed her own fingers across the top of his shoulders, enjoying the feel of his muscles as their kisses deepened. His desire was growing; she knew by the firm urgency in his hands, the hunger that needed to be satisfied. How she longed to throw caution to the wind, to drown in the feelings she was experiencing; but years of emptiness, of loving and then being rejected, acted as a brake on her emotions.

She pulled away, placing her trembling hands on his heaving chest; her breath was as ragged as his and she avoided his eyes, keeping her head lowered. His hands still rested on her back with a familiarity that caused equal amounts of pain and pleasure. She raised her head, unable to face him with a false look of composure; she was too agitated even to pretend.

'Kate,' he murmured huskily, his voice still warm with a slumberous unspoken invitation.

She smiled wanly and shook her head. 'Goodnight, Sebastian,' she said firmly, swallowing the painful swell of emotion that formed in her throat.

For a moment he hesitated and she felt a twirl of panic. She knew she no longer had the strength to fight him, to hide the depth of her feelings for him. They stood in silence for what seemed like an eternity to Kate before Sebastian spoke.

'Goodnight, Katy,' he said softly, the click of the door echoing in the the room as a sad reminder of how alone she now was.

CHAPTER TEN

KATE groaned softly as she forced her eyelids open.
She blinked as the bright light of early dawn stung her
eyes. She rubbed her forehead; a faint dull throb
drummed as she tried to remember last night's events.

Her eyes shot open, her hand flying to her face, and
she trailed her fingertips over her soft lips. A flush of
colour covered her face as she recalled all the details
of last night. Many of them were hazy flashes of
incidents, but the moment she had entered her room
was crystal-clear.

He had kissed her. The smile that curled Kate's lips
faded as the cool realisation of what had happened
next began to sink in. How on earth was she to face
him today? No doubt it had all been her fault. Her
behaviour had been a direct result of the hot sun and
drinking too much. Even the few beers she had had
were far more than her usual. The alcohol had given
her the edge of courage she had needed to deal with
Sebastian but now she was totally embarrassed.

The thought of facing him was awful but Kate was
determined to retain as much dignity as she could. She
had a quick shower, dressed simply for the day's
excursion, then threw her few remaining clothes into
her case.

Breakfast was served buffet-style and consisted
mainly of fresh fruit: mangoes, melons and pineapples,
with an abundance of steaming, strong Kenyan coffee.

A cooked meal was available as well, but Kate certainly didn't feel up to it. She helped herself to some warm bread and made her way over to the table where Sebastian sat staring out across the bush, oblivious to her arrival. She paused, then took a steadying breath; she was determined to brazen it out.

'Hello,' she said quietly, too self-conscious to say anything more till she could read his reaction.

'Good morning, Kate.' His voice was low and controlled and his face an expressionless mask. Kate pulled back her chair; it scraped noisily on the floor, making her grimace. 'Headache?' he drawled, reading her expression. Kate looked at him, annoyed by his taunting smile.

'No! Not. . .really,' she said, concentrating on her plate to avoid his penetrating gaze.

'Coffee will help,' he acknowledged, filling her cup; the aroma was a welcome stimulant.

'Thanks. I don't usually drink more than a glass of wine. I was just so thirsty last night after the heat of the day,' she added by way of explanation, or maybe defence, she thought ruefully as she buttered her bread, glad of some activity. 'I'm sorry if I. . .' Her voice trailed off.

'Can't you remember?' he cajoled, his long, tapering fingers toying with his cup while he kept his eyes fixed firmly on her.

Kate exhaled softly then glanced up, smiling halfheartedly. She ran a hand through her hair, unconsciously fluffing it into a soft cloud. 'Parts,' she confessed. She refused to comment about last night. He probably wanted to forget all about it, to put it down to her immaturity again.

'Like limboing under the table?' Sebastian offered helpfully, but his voice held a teasing softness.

Kate laughed nervously. 'I didn't,' she protested, raising her head swiftly then holding it still as it caused her a sudden sharp pain.

'No, you didn't,' he assured her with a smile that fanned the flame of desire he had awoken in her last night and which still hadn't died. Kate allowed herself to join in his laughter. It helped to defuse the situation.

'I never drink beer at all normally and certainly never that amount,' she told him. She gave a sheepish smirk. She picked up her coffee and grimaced as the bitter taste hit the back of her throat.

'It's just as well,' commented Sebastian coolly with a measure of censure in his tone. 'No wonder you can't remember, or is your memory being a little selective?' he asked in a seductive drawl that warned Kate she was treading on thin ice and had to be very careful.

'I can remember,' she answered emphatically, draining her coffee-cup and pouring herself another. She felt she needed it: the caffeine might stimulate her brain into some rapid thinking. 'It's just hazy,' she faltered, trying to sound casual and unperturbed by his line of questioning.

He raised his eyebrows, the hint of a smile playing about the corners of his mouth.

'OK, I remember,' she snapped, no longer wanting him to play this cat-and-mouse game with her emotions. 'I kissed you,' she said with calculated indifference. 'So what? I had a little too much to drink and it just happened. It was no big deal,' she concluded, hating the lie but knowing she had to appear unruffled by last night's events if she had any chance of surviving today. Why didn't he contradict her, tell her it was important, that the alcohol had only helped them both to express how they truly felt? Instead he remained totally impassive.

'No big deal,' he agreed, his expression guarded, but his eyes took on a cold, haunted look that chilled Kate's blood. He pushed his breakfast plate away from him in sudden disgust, as if he had lost all his appetite. He picked up his cup and knocked back the last dregs of coffee in a fashion that made Kate wonder if he felt like something stronger. She shifted her gaze away, taking a firm interest in her half-eaten breakfast and feigning indifference to his action while internally she was all at sea.

'I'll just go and check my room,' she told him in a calm, controlled tone of voice. 'Just to see if I've left anything,' she added as she stood up and moved away. She wanted to be out of his presence. He stood as she left, forever the perfect gentleman.

Nothing had changed; nothing would *ever* change between them. This latest incident was just another of the silly childish slips that he expected from her. Kate was so angry with herself for allowing it to happen. But surely he had responded? she mused as she picked up her case and wandered outside.

The sky was a cloudless blue, the sun already a golden disc in the sky. Kate sighed as her eyes scanned over the bush; it was beautiful and not even last night's unfortunate incident was going to spoil it. It was only a kiss, like others stolen from him years before, yet in some way, it was different. Kate couldn't comprehend the change but she knew it and sensed it as only a woman could.

'All aboard,' called the guide, breaking into her thoughts, as he walked past and clambered into the open-topped Jeep. She picked up her case and sauntered after him. The luggage was transported on a separate vehicle while they went off in search of the wildlife. Kate made her way to the back of the Jeep, settling herself down and trying to remain immune to Sebastian's presence—but he was already waiting for her. He smiled and shifted up in his seat as she approached.

'Feeling better?' he asked.

'No!' Her denial was as fast and quick as the look she flashed at him, but not so quick that he did not see the troubled pain in her eyes. 'A little groggy, that's all,' she said, trying to cover her discomfort.

'Good,' he replied curtly, lowering his sunglasses.

The incessant talking of the guide filled the following empty, embarrassed silence which developed between them. It was interesting to learn, as they drove past the herds of zebras, that the animals' stripes baffled tsetse flies; somehow it made rising at the crack of dawn worthwhile. Nervous antelope scattered at the first sound of the engine, darting between the scrub bush into the gauzy acacia trees, then off into the far distance. The Jeep drew to a halt to allow the tourists to take photographs, or just watch the antics of the elephants.

'It's a pity so many are hunted,' Kate said, horrified by the details of the poachers who were systematically killing elephants with no thought of the future.

'The black market in ivory and furs is extremely lucrative,' Sebastian remarked drily, re-focusing his camera to take another shot. He leaned over towards

Kate to take the picture and at that moment she chose to turn, her face only inches away from his. He lowered his camera, a smile tugging at the corner of his lips. Kate flushed as his warm breath caressed her face and she quickly lowered her lids to conceal the interest she knew would blaze there despite her efforts to prevent it. Sebastian pushed her shoulder, moving her out of his line of vision, his touch causing a sudden, unexpected twirl of excitement in her stomach.

'Just lean back while I take this shot,' he told her briskly, and then began snapping away and rolling the film on with skilful ease. Kate sat savouring the effect that his close proximity was having on her, feelings that she knew she could no longer deny.

'Thanks, that was great; magnificent beasts, aren't they? Tragic that they could become extinct.' Sebastian sat back, his thigh stiffening slightly as it brushed against Kate's, and he hesitated for a moment.

'Money, money, money! People are obsessed with it,' said Kate disgustedly as she looked at the small elephant calf hiding under the legs of its mother.

'My, you've changed your tune,' said Sebastian, surprised by the conviction in Kate's voice. 'You used to be the credit-card queen!'

Kate bristled, but his words were true. 'I suppose I was,' she admitted. 'I never gave a thought to anything.'

'Why the change?' he asked. She picked up the genuine warmth and interest in his voice and responded to it. Her heart knocked against her ribs as he picked up her hands in his strong fingers. 'Come on, Kate, why the change?'

'When I decided to stand on my own two feet I was

quite determined not to use my allowance, so I was forced to live on my small income and—surprise!' she said, laughing at herself. 'I managed.' Her pride in herself was evident. Sebastian still had hold of her hand, resting it on his knee with an ease that made it seem so comfortable and natural.

'Hence the grubby flat?' he said, still remembering Terry, but nodding understandingly.

'It wasn't grubby, it was perfectly clean,' Kate cried, hurt by his unfounded criticism.

'All right, calm down!' He grinned, giving her hand an affectionate squeeze and sending an electric volt through her body.

'I'm very proud of that flat. . .'

'Are you?'

'Yes. I achieved that on my own. *On my own*,' she repeated. 'Do you know what that means?' she said, facing him squarely with a mixture of indignation and pride.

'You mean without just being accepted into the family business?'

'No, I wasn't making any gibe at you. I was forced to make it on my own terms and I'm grateful for that,' she told him, realising for the first time that being independent had helped her to mature.

'Forced?' repeated Sebastian. 'What do you mean, forced?'

Kate inwardly acknowledged that she should have chosen her words more carefully; Sebastian was too sharp.

'Nothing,' she said quickly—too quickly—turning away and dragging her hand from his. She couldn't tell him. To admit it to herself was painful enough, without having to explain to Sebastian about her father's rejection.

'Come on, Kate,' he said in a deep, coaxing voice. 'I know you too well. Tell me,' he insisted.

She was trying desperately not to be affected by his nearness and her response was defensively curt.

'Forget it!' she snapped, feeling terribly threatened by him and by her own desire to share her troubles. She had to put an end to this conversation before she revealed too much.

'Kate. . .' His voice, though quiet, held an unmistakable steely edge that alerted her to his determination to know the truth. She hesitated; she was too aware of the scenes that had led up to her father's rejection of her; she remembered how much a part of those rows Sebastian had been. She took a slow, calming breath as she tried to keep her emotions under control.

'I'm not bothered now. It's in the past and I have a new life,' she began to explain, but Sebastian cut in, his patience at an end.

'There's something you're not telling me, Kate, isn't there?' he persisted. 'I've known there was something wrong ever since I picked you up from the hospital,' he added in a gentler tone.

Kate lowered her head and knew there was no turning back now, so she plunged on.

'I did want to come home,' she confessed in a small voice. 'But I never received any answers to my letters, so I guessed. . .' Her mouth dried and she cast a covert glance at Sebastian to gauge his reaction to her admission.

'Kate, are you sure?'

'Sure? Of course I'm sure!' she cried indignantly, her pain veering towards anger that he did not believe her. 'Have you any idea how lonely I was?' The expression on her face was etched with the fine pen of painful experience.

'Oh, Kate,' Sebastian said sadly. 'You should have come home. Talked to me.'

'I couldn't. I left under such a dark cloud. And when I received no reply to my letters I decided to make it on my own,' she informed him, suddenly feeling better now that she had explained her behaviour to him.

'And you succeeded?' he asked doubtfully. All he knew was that she had been living with a man who no doubt paid all the bills, which he thought was so typical of Kate. He didn't realise she had built up a career with the charity.

'Yes—yes, I did,' agreed Kate readily. 'Humble though it was, that was my flat—all mine.' Her soft mouth widened into a tempting smile.

'So what is this job of yours that has brought about such a change?' he asked coolly. 'You haven't joined some weird religious sect, have you?' He gave a wicked grin that made her heart soar as the last few barriers she had built to protect herself against him began to fall.

'No, I haven't!' Her laughter carried on the early morning air, stirring him with its lightness. 'It's called job satisfaction and it has nothing to do with how much one is paid,' she told him firmly. She watched his winged dark brows rise playfully at her words.

'So what do you do?' he queried, intrigued by her genuine conviction about her work and recognising that it meant a great deal to her.

'I work for a Third World charity,' she began as she caught the flicker of surprise and approval in his dark eyes. 'I'm a co-ordinator,' she explained, seeing his frown when he didn't understand. 'Developing overseas projects, working as a go-between. I sort out whether or not the idea is viable, then arrange the finance.'

'I'm impressed! It sounds interesting,' he acknowledged, with a slight inclination of his head, and Kate warmed to her topic. At last he was proud of her and she had something to boast about.

'We're not an aid agency, though obviously we do offer emergency help when required—unfortunately too often; but most of our funds are directed into long-term projects. Our aim is to aid development through education.'

'I see,' he said, sounding distant, as if he was thinking about something else. 'And your father knows nothing of this work, I presume, even though you told him in your letters?'

'I've told him about my work but I've never mentioned the letters.' She shrugged, trying to appear indifferent to her pain. 'It's not worth it now. It's no longer important.'

'Good. You're probably right to forget about it,' he agreed. 'Any projects in this area?' he asked. His question was casual enough, but Kate sensed a deeper motive than just curiosity, but her own desire to tell him about some of her projects made her fail to challenge him.

'I've worked on several through the Mombasa office, but I doubt I will ever see the results of all my efforts— everything is too long-term.' She sighed. It was some-

times so hard to put such effort into a project and yet
see nothing for it.

'Maybe you could do with a change—quick turn-
overs, instant profits, results at the end of each day?'
he encouraged, sensing her despair. Kate shrugged;
she had the satisfaction of knowing she was helping
people, but the quick thrill, the sudden buzz that her
father's business could generate was not there.

'I don't know,' she admitted. 'I don't even know
whether I'd be able to cope with the cut and thrust
now.' There was a haunting, plaintive strain in her
voice, telling of chances missed.

Quirking a teasing grin, he eyed her. 'Coward!' he
chided mildly.

She bristled at his accusation, even if it was meant
in jest. Kate knew her limitations but she was no
coward. She sometimes had to fight like a bear to get
some projects off the ground.

'No, I'm not,' she retorted. 'I'm surprised that you
said that,' she added, in a light tone to show that she
was not really offended.

'So there's no chance of you joining the family
business?' Sebastian challenged, his tone serious, and
Kate suddenly knew he meant that the thing she had
wanted all her life was now casually being offered to
her.

'Is that an offer?' she asked, trying to keep the
excitement from her voice.

'I feel we could certainly use someone like you now
that we are to diversify.' Sebastian's words were persuasive and flattering, but Kate wasn't sure.

'I don't think so—big business is no longer for me,'
she concluded, not wanting to tell him of her fears that

if she worked with him she would be totally vulnerable to him again.

'Why not?'

'I haven't the motivation any more.'

'What motivation?'

'To make money,' she said simply, turning to face him. She scanned his angular face as he remained silent.

'Do you think that's the major concern?' he asked after a while.

'Isn't it?' Kate quickly rejoined.

'Kate!' He was shocked, and that took her by surprise. It wasn't anger he was showing—he was hurt. 'You know me better than that. I enjoy work, though not as much as your father.' Sebastian added this last piece quickly, knowing how Kate felt about her father's workaholic tendencies. 'And, yes, I'd rather be a little rich than a little poor—who wouldn't?' he argued.

'I'm sorry. You're right; I'm afraid I've become a little self-righteous. It's just that I see the results of our desire for wealth—the damage we cause,' she told him with a heartfelt sigh.

'I know, Kate; that's why a change might do you good,' Sebastian offered again, noting the doubt that was still present in her mind.

'I'll consider your offer. Is that all right?' She couldn't commit herself yet; there was too much to contemplate.

Sebastian grasped her hand, holding it tightly but tenderly, and stroked his fingers across her smooth skin. Kate looked down, following the languid movements of his fingers.

'I meant it, Kate!' Sebastian's smoky voice took on a slumberous warmth. 'We could really use someone like you. You've an instinct for figures for a start,' he drawled, increasing the pressure of his fingers as he spoke, and sending a shudder of longing spiralling through Kate's body. 'And you've obviously gained an excellent knowledge of Third World economics and problems.'

'It would be fun working together,' she managed, her voice coming out in an unattractive squeak as she tried to remain immune to his electric touch. Her cheeks pinkened with self-consciouness and she kept her head lowered to prevent him from seeing the effect it was having on her.

'You bet!' he agreed firmly, before adding softly, 'I'd make sure of that.'

'His certainty unnerved her. The words were inno-cent enough, but there was a definite implication in them that disturbed Kate almost more than she was prepared to admit. She turned her attention back to the bush, totally aware of his hand still holding hers and accepting how good it felt. She tried to listen to the guide, tried to take an interest in the amusing antics of the wart-hogs and the beautiful scenes that were passing in front of her eyes—marvellous wildlife only feet away from her—but her mind was concen-trating on one thought alone: Sebastian. Could she work with him? How did he really feel about her? Would it be a total disaster if she returned to the family business? The questions were endless and yet there was no solution.

They arrived at the lodges by midday, just as the

sun was becoming unbearably hot. The shimmering swimming-pool that curved in an ingenious abstract shape seemed to beckon everyone.

'Fancy a swim?' asked Sebastian, inclining his head to the tempting water—not that Kate needed an invitation: she had already made up her own mind to go in.

'I'll be down in less than five minutes,' she nodded, snatching up her case and taking the stairs two at a time. In her room, she pulled the swimsuit from her case and viewed it doubtfully; she couldn't imagine now what had possessed her to buy such a revealing outfit—it left little to the imagination.

But the sound of splashing water that came through the open French windows made her throw caution to the wind. She quickly shed her clothes and pulled on her vivid orange costume. Lightly she ran her fingers over the sleek Lycra material; the high-cut legs emphasised her slim hips and flat stomach, before her shape rounded up and out to her firm, erect breasts which the costume's plunging neckline revealed—far more than she wanted! She pulled at the straps but it made little difference—the costume kept springing back to its original shape. There was only one thing for it: she had to be in the water before Sebastian, so she raced downstairs quickly and made her way to the pool.

She dived neatly in. The rush of cold water that covered her was wonderful, waking every part of her. She surfaced, catching hold of the side of the pool before pushing back her hair till it was smooth against her head. Her face was shown to perfection: her wide, bright eyes with their pensive depths, the softness of her golden skin and the fullness of her mouth as her lips gently curled to smile at Sebastian, who had entered the pool only seconds after her. She caught his reaction—a flicker of sexual interest in her—as it flashed across his face, his pupils dilating slightly as he looked intently at her.

'Race you?' he grinned as he swam nearer. Their bodies moved slightly against each other in the cool waters and his thighs momentarily touched hers. Kate was aware of his closeness and her own desire to move even nearer to him; she was enjoying the sensation he was arousing and could feel his response to her.

'Don't be childish,' she pretended to scold him, not wanting to destroy the dangerous but exciting atmosphere that was bubbling up between them.

'Frightened you'll lose?' The challenge was bright in his dark eyes as they dropped from her face to the soft cleavage of her breasts. Kate followed his gaze, her blood heating and rushing through her veins.

'No, I was always a better swimmer than you and I've youth on my side,' she said playfully.

'Rubbish!' he cried, raising his hand to tuck a stray lock of hair behind her ear. Kate sucked in her breath. It was one thing teasing, quite another touching, and she felt her insides melt. She instinctively moved her head to avoid his touch but instead it made his fingers caress her cheek.

'I thought you would outgrow your competitive streak,' she said quickly, trying to hide the depth of feeling he was stirring in her.

'Never!' he vowed. 'But if you're chicken. . .?' he teased her.

Kate needed no further goading; besides, she wanted to put some distance between them, to escape to safety.

'Go!' she said, and she set off, cutting through the water and racing for the other end of the pool with dogged determination. She could hear Sebastian gaining on her and pushed herself even further; her heart soared as her hand slapped down on the far side of the pool.

'Winner!' she panted, her breath coming out in an exhausted whisper.

'Cheat!' complained Sebastian, laughing, his white teeth gleaming against his bronzed skin, which dripped with water.

'You're just a sore loser,' Kate grinned, her breath steadying now but her heart still thudding painfully against her chest as their bodies were pushed together with the force of water, their legs becoming momentarily tangled.

'You started before me,' he reminded her.

'Only just.'

'Precisely,' he said as he pushed her head firmly under the water. Kate kicked frantically before choking her way back to the surface. She stretched her hand out, determined to exact revenge and duck Sebastian, but he was much too quick for her. He trapped her wrists in a tight grip, drawing her close so that their wet bodies slammed against each other. Taken by surprise, Kate had no time to draw away from the inevitable kiss—not that she would have done; she ached for him! He lowered his mouth to hers and she reached to meet his lips. The intensity of their kiss deepened and the gnawing hunger that needed to be satiated threatened to overwhelm them. Kate was afraid of losing control so she reluctantly drew back, pushing Sebastian away. Her expression tightened as the excitement of the moment began to subside. She looked at him, the doubts and fears and confusion shining out in her eyes.

'I think I'll get out now,' she told him, turning away, her voice as shaky as her limbs as she climbed out of the pool.

He watched her. She could feel his heated gaze on her back and she was conscious again of the figure-hugging style of her swimsuit. It was like history repeating itself. All the old emotions were rushing up, hitting her head and heart full-on, and she could do nothing to prevent it. She wasn't even sure she wanted to. The offer of working for the family firm only compounded her problems. She longed to work in her father's company but she had real commitment to her charity. Besides, was it wise to consider working so closely with Sebastian? Was she reading too much into his kisses? She had made a fool of herself once before like that and wasn't about to do so again.

Back in her room, Kate stood under the shower, letting the warm water cover her body, washing away the tension that was tightening every strained nerve in her body. She knew she could no longer fool herself, despite all her promises; the simple fact was that she loved him, had always loved him and no doubt always would. The realisation filled her more with a sick feeling of dread than joy, and she dressed with a heavy heart.

The sharp rap on the door startled her, breaking into her thoughts. She opened it, surprised to see Sebastian. He normally waited downstairs for her.

'Come in,' she gasped. 'I won't be a minute.' She walked over to the dressing-table, applied her lipstick, then picked up her bag and room-key. 'Ready!' She smiled brightly. She was dreading this evening and was glad that they would be driving back to Mombasa tomorrow. She didn't know how much longer she could take being in his company in this relaxed way.

The hotel's restaurant was already busy, with waiters moving agilely between tables, producing plates of delicious food with a flourish. Kate sat down, toying nervously with her napkin. It was too intimate—the low lights, the flickering flames of candlelight and the soft music that wafted on the sweet-scented night air.

'I've ordered champagne,' Sebastian announced, his voice holding a warmth that made her stomach flip.

'Champagne?' she queried. 'Are we celebrating?'

'Yes, we are,' he said, taking the bottle from the bucket at the side of the table and expertly wrapping a cloth around it in one graceful swirl. 'Your return to the family business.' He filled her glass. Kate watched the bubbles rise to a foamy white top before picking up the glass and tasting it—it was delicious!

'I haven't said I will yet,' she parried, flicking the top of her tongue over her softly parted lips. She was conscious of the tension that had sprung between them.

'But you will,' he coaxed, a wicked gleam in his eyes. Kate gave him a faintly amused look, her eyebrows rising.

'Will I?' she challenged him, warming to the easy banter.

'Of course! I can be very persuasive.' His voice was taking on a low, sexy growl.

'Really?' Kate came back, peeping at him over the

rim of her crystal glass, sending out messages that she knew he would respond to.

'Let's eat,' he replied, grinning, settling back as a plate full of delicately cut pieces of charcoal-cooked chicken was put before him.

'The wine and food have been marvellous, haven't they?' Kate commented. 'Far better than I would have imagined possible,' she said, popping a tiny sliver of fresh coconut into her mouth.

'Not to mention the quality of the beer,' he reminded her with a laugh.

Kate coloured and confessed sheepishly, as she recalled her behaviour, 'Those beers are deadly.'

'So it would seem,' Sebastian teased in that familiar way that made her legs weaken.

The meal was lovely and Kate enjoyed it, despite the slight tension that tightened her stomach.

'Would you care to dance?' Sebastian said when they had finished, putting down his coffee-cup and looking at her with a quizzical expression. She hesitated for a moment, knowing how deadly his proximity could be.

'Of course,' she agreed, pushing back her chair.

The music was slow—too slow, Kate thought; it forced their bodies to move in a seductive harmony and she was too aware of the way her own mutinous body seemed to push against his hips. In her head she wanted to dance apart, to move around in a fast, uncluttered way that would not enforce any intimacy. But Sebastian swayed to and fro, gently taking her with him, their bodies pressed up against each other and her soft breasts resting on his hard, muscular chest. The music never seemed to end and Kate wasn't even sure she wanted it to. It seemed so natural, their bodies moving like a well-orchestrated ballet, dancing with a familiarity that only served to awaken other, latent desires.

'I'm enjoying this, aren't you?' murmured Sebastian.

Kate knew he could sense her reluctance to let go. He pressed his hand into her back, drawing her even closer while moving his hips against her till Kate gave a small cry of shock and pleasure.

'Kate,' he whispered, her name like a lover's incantation on his lips, and his body melted into hers. She reached out for him; her hands smoothed over his shoulders, her fingers speaking all the emotions she felt without breaking the magic of the silence with pointless words. She didn't know how it happened—it just did. One minute they were on the dance-floor, the next they were taking the stairs to her room. It felt so right. Gone were any last lingering doubts. She knew he wanted her, saw her as an equal. This was the moment she had dreamed of and it seemed so natural.

A cool breeze blew through the opened window and yellow moonlight spilt across the floor. She turned to face him and as the door clicked closed they moved into each other's arms, then fell on to the bed.

The bright light of a new day poured through the unshuttered windows and fell across the love-tossed sheets. The fine mosquito net cast a shimmering shadow on the two tightly entwined bodies that were curled up against each other, locked in a lovers' embrace.

Kate stirred, stretching a little. She raised her head

and let her cheek nuzzle against the dark patch of tight curls that covered Sebastian's chest. She leaned into his solidness, enjoying the feel of his naked body against hers, delighting in its supple strength. He moved, pulling her in closer and wrapping a possessive arm around her waist. Kate shifted round so that she could see his face, perhaps to read the regret that she was afraid might be in his eyes. But when she turned to meet his dark blue gaze she wondered at the love she saw there. She lifted her hands to the wide expanse of his shoulders, her hips grazing his, sparking the flame of desire.

'I love you,' she whispered, her voice coming out in a sexy whisper. She ran her fingers though his hair, inhaling the fresh smell of him. Her smile held a measure of insecurity as he seemed unprepared to reaffirm the words that had sprung so readily to his lips last night.

But, 'I love you too,' he suddenly murmured, his lips gently moving across hers, then ranging lower across her neck and throat. Feeling a fresh surge of desire, Kate encircled his body with her arms, her fingers seeking and searching, exploring every inch of him, carefully storing each minute detail in her mind and heart. She had longed to hear those words; she couldn't remember a time in her life when she hadn't longed for them. This was her dream come true. It was almost unbelievable.

She started to stroke his hair, smoothing it back from his face so that she could see every inch of him, to reassure herself that he was here with her and in love. He began to stroke her thigh, sending a spiral of excitement through her slightly trembling body. His movements were slow, carefully light, arousing her to dizzy heights. He trailed a delicate row of kisses over her shoulders, then lower till he reached the swelling peak of her breast. Kate gave a gasp of pure pleasure, before her breath was trapped in a vortex of delight. She fell on to her back, her arms reaching out and pulling him towards her. She sank her fingers deep into his broad shoulders, clinging to him as she soared higher and higher into heightened passion.

Finally, when she could no longer endure the overwhelming sensations, she released herself totally with a cry of rapture, before slowly sinking back to rest on his rapidly moving chest, which was shimmering with the visible signs of his exertion. They stayed locked together, Kate contentedly sheltering in the crook of his arm, her eyes half closed as she revelled in the luxury of being in love with the only man who had ever mattered to her.

It was with great reluctance that she finally dragged herself away from him, but she longed for a cool, refreshing shower before they faced the long trip back to Mombasa.

The bush was always full of mystery and excitement, but for Kate, today, the colours were more vibrant, the sky a clearer, brighter blue than ever before, and the animals examples of perfect form and beauty. Sebastian held her hand, his thumb gently stroking over hers as if he would never let her go.

'It will be so much fun, won't it?' he said. 'Together again and you joining the family firm.'

Kate turned to smile at him and she nodded. She knew now that her working days for the charity were numbered and she was about to begin a new and exciting part of her life—with Sebastian.

'I can't wait, but I wonder how Daddy is going to react—and your mother?' she said, suddenly anxious.

'Delighted, I'm sure,' Sebastian told her firmly, drawing her back in his arms, and she settled down, confident that everything was going to be all right.

The villa was empty when they returned.

'They must have gone out for the day,' Sebastian said, returning to Kate who stood waiting in the hall. The look of disappointment on her face was palpable. 'It's all right. We can tell them the good news tonight.'

Kate nodded in agreement. It was so hard not to scream the news from the rooftops!

'I'm going back into town. There's some work I really must see to,' Sebastian explained, lightly planting a kiss on Kate's cheek.

'I'll come,' Kate said, dreading the thought of them being apart. 'I can go to the charity offices in Mombasa. I'd like to see some of my projects in action,' she continued, failing to see the dark shadow that fell across Sebastian's face.

'Don't you think you'd best stay here?' he argued. 'For when your father gets back,' he added as an extra incentive.

Kate shook her head firmly, feeling disappointed that Sebastian seemed reluctant to take her along.

'All right, come on,' he said, extending his hand, but Kate sensed he was unhappy with her decision.

He dropped her off in the main square and Kate said she would take a cab back home as neither of them knew how long they would be. She went and looked round the spartan charity offices—a complete contrast with hers in London. There was no computer, no fax-machine or photocopier, just a couple of very old desks and an old Bakelite telephone. The filing system consisted of an assortment of cardboard boxes and the charts on the paint-peeling walls were yellowed with sunlight and age. Kate listened attentively as Moses, her Kenyan co-worker, gave her a full commentary on all her work. She felt a stab of regret as she left the small bungalow building and realised she would never be part of that team again.

'Allan!' she cried in surprise as she recognised the familiar face. 'How are you?'

'Kate. How delightful. What are you doing here?' he asked in surprise, nodding to the building she had just come out of.

'It's where I work—at least I work for its counterpart in England,' she explained.

'How marvellous! Such good work but so frustrating. I'm still struggling with local officials but it would seem that Duplas win the day,' he said regretfully, shaking his head.

'Duplas?' asked Kate, something stirring in her memory.

'You remember I told you about them? They are opening a plant here. It is bad for the people, bad for the environment, but I can do nothing,' he said in a resigned tone.

'Maybe I could help through the charity,' Kate said hurriedly, hating to see his disappointment, and the thought of this company so blatantly exploiting the area.

'I fear, Kate, it's too late. The man from Duplas

signed the final papers only moments ago. Yet another victory for free enterprise,' he added bitterly.

Duplas, Duplas, Duplas: the name rang through Kate's mind. She had heard it somewhere, but couldn't quite place it.

'Kate, Kate, what is it? Are you ill?' demanded Allan, watching in horror as all the colour drained from Kate's face. Now she recalled where she had heard the name before! Her head was swimming as she tried to focus her mind. It couldn't be true—not Sebastian; he wouldn't, would he? she questioned herself, remembering just how ambitious Sebastian was. No wonder he hadn't wanted her father to know of his plans to diversify. Howard would never have agreed to such a plan!

'I'm fine. Fine. It must be the heat,' she pretended. 'Just get me a cab, Allan. I'll be OK,' she reassured him, her voice gaining conviction and strength as she thought of Sebastian's betrayal. Her mind was in a turmoil. She didn't want to believe it, but the facts were all falling neatly into place. After years of convincing her she wasn't ready to join her father's company, he'd finally offered her a position only when he'd learned of her Third World work and was obviously frightened she would find out about his intentions—as indeed she had.

Kate felt a rush of colour to her face. She had been such a fool, falling for his masterly seduction when all he wanted was to have her safely ensconced in the family business where she could do no harm! As a member of the company she would be forced to agree to his diversification plans no matter how much they went against her principles.

'Sebastian! Sebastian!' she yelled, the moment she entered the front door of the villa. She was determined to face him straight away.

The door to the office opened and she spun around, the bitter taste of betrayal and humiliation burning her throat.

'Kate?' queried Louisa, her face troubled. 'Is there something wrong?'

'Where's Sebastian?' snapped Kate, her eyes burning with hot, unshed tears.

'I'm afraid he's not here at the moment. He has gone to town to sign some papers.'

'Has he?' Kate said with an ironic tone.

'He's just telephoned through. He also told me you were returning to the family business.' Louisa smiled too sweetly, but Kate was far too lost in her own emotions to catch the sound of panic rising in Louisa's voice.

'No, never!' she bit back, knowing that she could never do that, not now. 'Louisa,' she said, a dull realisation coming over her, 'you deal with all the company correspondence, don't you?'

Louisa looked troubled as she shuffled a sheaf of papers in her hands, her fingers moving agitatedly over the edges.

'Not all,' she said quietly.

'Then who does?' Kate demanded, knowing now why her father had never answered her letters—he had never received them.

'Sebastian,' Louisa told her. Her eyes remained fixed on her papers; she didn't raise her head to face Kate, who nodded to herself. It was the final piece in the jigsaw. It had been Sebastian all along, keeping her apart from her father. She should have known! How love can put blinkers over your eyes, Kate thought sadly, suddenly feeling drained.

'I think I'll go and lie down,' she told Louisa. 'I'll see Sebastian later,' she added, surprised by the venom in her tone as she said his name.

But she couldn't rest, despite the throbbing in her head and dull ache in her heart. She felt such a fool. After all this time she should have known that Sebastian didn't really care for her. Yet part of her so desperately wanted to believe that there was some mistake, and that some simple explanation would clear him of any guilt.

The moment Kate heard his car she rushed downstairs, eager to face him and to know the truth. Inwardly she was praying that he was innocent, that he did truly love her. She rushed down, breathless with exertion. Sebastian looked up, frowning when he saw her.

'Kate, what is it?' he demanded, seeing the distraught look in her eyes, the bright gleam that warned him something was wrong.

'I want to know about the Duplas deal,' she told him, facing him squarely. Her outward manner was tough, despite how she felt inside.

Sebastian stiffened. 'We'd better discuss this in private.' His words hung in the air as he made his way into the study.

'Now, what's all this about, Kate?' he said softly, closing the door behind them. His hands came up to rest on her arms but Kate moved away. She knew how his touch affected her and she wanted the whole truth first. His brow creased, confusion and anger flitting across his face.

'I've spoken to Allan Doran today,' she said. 'He told me all about the deal.'

'Told you what?' Sebastian's anger was growing now on equal pace to Kate's, and they stood facing each other, fury welling up between them. Kate delighted in his reaction. She had hit her mark and, though it hurt, she still pressed on, her anger and her sense of bitter betrayal urging her to show him how strong she was.

'About the deal, the effects the plant will have on the environment and the people.' The contempt in her voice was now evident, and the scorn on her face added to the cutting edge of her words. 'And how he tried to stop it. . .'

'And you believe him?' demanded Sebastian, taking hold of her upper arms in a tight, strong grip, forcing her to look at him.

'Well, it does explain a lot, doesn't it?' Kate jeered, longing to hear him deny her accusation—but he didn't.

'Does it?'

'Yes, it does,' she snapped back, hating the hard grip he had on her, which was bereft of any of the tenderness he had shown the night before. 'You didn't want to share details of the Duplas plan, and you certainly didn't want me back, did you?' She didn't wait for a reply. Her own sense of lost love was urging her on. 'You know, I could never understand why Daddy never replied to my letters, but now I do. It was you, wasn't it? You were determined to make sure I stayed away so you could implement your plans——'

'No, Kate!' he cut in, his grip tightening further.

'Yes!' she cried. 'You wanted to make sure your plans to diversify went ahead without any hitches, but because of my charity work I might have found out, become a threat, and you couldn't stand the thought of that.'

'I don't know what you're talking about! Listen to me; let me explain.' His voice was calmer now, more in control, but the throb of a nerve at his temple warned her that he was barely keeping his temper in check.

'No, *you* listen! These people are poor—desperately poor—and, yes, they want work. But you're taking advantge of that—paying them a pittance while you make huge profits!'

Kate paused, then shook herself free. She saw the stung, hurt look on Sebastian's face but her own personal pain was greater. 'You disgust me,' she spat out at him.

'You're not even prepared to listen, are you?' he growled, his eyes diamond-hard chips. 'You've already condemned me.'

There was a kind of sorrow in his voice that she had not expected.

'Then why won't you deny it?' she asked, her tone filled with a desperate plea. She longed to hear him tell her it was all a mistake but he remained silent, just looking at her.

'Why should I?' he finally retorted, his voice as cold as the icy look on his face. 'You already know the truth, don't you, Kate?' he taunted, and, with that, he turned on his heel and left her alone in the study. The faint scent of his aftershave hung in the air—the only sign that he had been there—and Kate had never felt so utterly alone in all her life.

Kate had been awake for hours. In fact she hadn't been sleeping properly for weeks. Terry had already left for work. He knew something was wrong and didn't want to pressurise her. He knew the type of work they did could put people under strain and he could see that the effects were evident in Kate.

She stared at the damp brown patch on the ceiling, the old, yellowing, peeling paint that only added to the dreariness of the room and her heavy, depressed mood. It was three months since her return from Kenya and she had not seen or heard from Sebastian since then.

Not that she wanted to, she reminded herself as she pushed off her quilt and tripped over to the bathroom. She cast an anxious glance at the calendar that was pinned to her door on the way. With each passing day the reality that she might be pregnant became stronger. She was dreading the weekend: it was her father's birthday and a family party had been arranged, one she knew she had to attend, but the thought of seeing Sebastian filled her with fear.

'Morning, Kate—you're in early,' called Terry, looking up from his papers as she arrived at the office. 'Moses has phoned from Mombasa. He said you'd asked him to look into something.'

'Yes—yes, I did,' Kate replied, showing the first sign of animation in months. Terry looked up at her, studying her features in detail.

'Don't get excited. He says he'll post the details.'

'Is that all?' Kate asked, her heart sinking, her shoulders sagging; and she suddenly felt drained again.

'No. He told me tell you that Duplas were in the clear. I don't know where you got your information from but Duplas are highly respectable. They're really concerned with positive development of the environment, and have no intention of exploiting the people or their resources.'

'I don't believe it!' Kate gasped, stunned by the news—and yet hadn't part of her known that? She had, in her heart of hearts, known that Sebastian was innocent.

She sighed, her mind whirling. Why hadn't he told her the truth? She just couldn't understand.

'Look, I don't know what this is all about,' Terry said. 'I don't want to know, I've enough to do, but I told you when you first began working here: don't get personally involved. This work is stressful enough, without adding to it.' He said this in a kindly way, looking at his young assistant with an air of sympathy.

'I'm all right,' Kate protested weakly.

'Kate, why not take a couple of days off? Go home early, have a rest and a good long think. Maybe this work is getting you down. Perhaps you need a change? A new direction, maybe—just what the doctor ordered?'

Kate nodded in reply. A long weekend certainly would perk her up and she knew she had to face Sebastian sooner or later—best to get it over with. Especially if she had to tell him she was pregnant. She couldn't imagine how he would react.

* * *

She had to travel to her family home by train—she still didn't have a car—and Clare had promised to pick her up at the station, but when Kate got there it was deserted. She scanned the car park, but Clare was not in sight.

'Kate!' Sebastian's abrupt tone cut through the still air, and she jumped in surprise as she turned to face him. He cast her a quick glance, frowning at the dark shadows under her eyes, before picking up her case and flinging it into the boot of his car. She climbed in, catching the stray scent of a heavy female perfume. Her heart knotted painfully in her chest. Was she jealous? No, of course not! She rolled down the window to rid the car of the sickly smell. Sebastian flashed her a curious look.

'How are you, Kate?' His voice was stiff, formally polite, and Kate knew she had to be as formal in return.

'Fine,' she lied unconvincingly. 'And yourself?' And so they made polite conversation all the way to the house. Kate hated it. She longed to mention the Duplas plant and her mistake, but the dark look in Sebastian's eyes made the words freeze on her lips.

Finally he drew the car to a halt outside the house, keeping the engine running.

'Aren't you coming in?' she asked when he remained seated, rapping his fingers impatiently on the steering-wheel.

'No, I'm due back at the office,' he informed her crisply, not even bothering to take his eyes off the road ahead.

'Oh.' Kate was disappointed. 'I was hoping to talk

to you. . .' Her heart fluttered as he turned his icy gaze on her.

'Were you?' he asked, puzzled. 'I can't imagine that we have anything to discuss—can you?' he added.

'Can I have my case?'

'Help yourself.'

'What a gentleman.'

'You know full well I'm not,' he returned.

'Sebastian. . .' Kate pleaded, longing to make amends, but his patience was at an end.

'I'm late, Kate. Hurry up!' he snapped, turning his attention back to the road.

Kate wasted no time. Tears were already theatening to fall as she pulled her case from the boot. She slammed it closed. The moment she did so Sebastian roared off, leaving her staring after him. She had ruined everything. There was nothing left between them now—only bitterness.

'Kate, darling!' Clare's warm welcome broke into her thoughts. Kate turned, forcing a smile on her face, but the smile was not genuine and anyone could see the sadness in her eyes.

'Come and sit down, Kate, and tell me what's going on with you and Sebastian,' said Clare briskly, ushering her inside.

'Me and Sebastian?' Kate echoed, trying to feign surprise, and failing.

'Yes, Kate.' Clare sighed wearily. 'He's been like a bear with a sore head since the holiday.'

'Has he?' Kate asked, trying to keep her emotions well-hidden in the deepest recesses of her mind.

'Were we wrong, Kate? We really thought if you

went on safari together——' Clare began, but Kate cut in, surprised by the revelation.

'That was deliberate?' She was nonplussed.

'Well, it could have easily been cancelled——'

'Then why wasn't it?' Kate interrupted her. It could have saved her from all this trouble!

Clare sighed again in frustration. 'Really, Kate,' she said exasperatedly. 'You and Sebastian have loved one another from the day you met, but you looked up to him far too much, and, believe me, that's no way for a relationship to last. My first marriage—to Sebastian's father—failed not because he was older than me, but because I changed, matured, wanted him to meet me on equal terms, and he couldn't.' She confessed this with a deep sigh of regret.

Kate said nothing. She had too much to think about. She stared at the floor and the intricate markings on the carpet.

'Kate, don't you see? That's why we wanted you to go away to school—to allow you to grow up. To allow Sebastian to have some other girlfriends, and to make sure you both knew what you were doing. And now what's happened? He's been refusing to go and see you. We thought you two were finally going to marry, despite Louisa's attempts to separate you.'

'Louisa?' Kate couldn't understand any more. Everything was totally different from how she had imagined it.

'Yes. Sebastian found out about her destroying your letters to your father. Silly girl! The truth will always come out in the end. Needless to say, she was sacked immediately. Sebastian wouldn't even let her work her notice.'

Clare continued talking, but Kate was no longer listening. She had been such a fool! Such a selfish *fool*! She had thought the worst of everyone and now she was paying a terrible price. She had to get away to sort her feelings out.

She rushed for the door. Clare was calling frantically after her, but she couldn't hear. She needed to be alone.

She ran down through the paddocks, longing to be in the stables, her secret childhood place whenever she'd needed to be by herself. She ignored the horses. Instead she climbed up high into the hayloft and lay in the sweet-smelling hay, hot tears splashing down her face. How could she have been such a fool? She had felt so rejected as a child that, when faced with love, she had been unable to recognise it. She had misjudged her father, and Clare, and her own feelings of insecurity had driven Sebastian away. She had never felt so miserable in all her life. She felt exhausted, emotionally drained. The hay was soft and warm, and her eyes, heavy with tears, finally closed.

'Kate.' The sound of her name pierced her consciousness. 'Kate.' Her name came again and she stiffened as she recognised the voice. She sat up, her eyes straining into the darkness. She could see the flash of a torch-light down below, flickering over the white-washed walls of the stables. The voice came again, sharper this time, and she knew she had to answer. She swallowed the dry lump that swelled in her throat.

'I'm here,' she said softly, suddenly embarrassed as Sebastian's head surfaced over the top of the ladder to the loft. 'I came to see the horses. I felt a little tired, so I must have fallen asleep,' she lied.

'Everyone wondered where you were, but I remembered,' he said, climbing up beside her.

'You remembered?' Kate repeated wistfully.

'I remembered,' he replied. 'I remember everything about you, Kate,' he added softly.

'Oh,' Kate gasped, a little stunned.

'Come on; we'd best go to dinner,' he said, moving towards the ladder.

'Sebastian, before we go. . . About Duplas. . .' Her voice slowly began to fade as he fixed his dark eyes on her. She took a steadying breath and continued, 'I know you're innocent. I should have trusted you.'

'Yes, you should,' he agreed.

'I'm sorry,' Kate said, her voice almost breaking with emotion.

'So am I.'

'But Allan was so convincing——'

'He would have been,' Sebastian cut in gruffly. 'The plant was offering such good wages that he was about to lose his poachers.'

'Poachers!' Kate gasped, unable to accept that she had been taken in so easily by his smooth charm. She shut her eyes to close her mind to the reality. 'I've been such an idiot, haven't I?'

'Yes,' agreed Sebastian, with a nod.

'I'm sorry,' she said, unable to think of anything else to say. She wanted to beg his forgiveness, to turn back the clock, but she knew that wasn't possible. There was no sign of forgiveness and her heart sank even further. 'I should have listened to you.'

She moved towards the ladder. There was nothing

left to say. Sebastian reached out, touching her upper arm. His grip was not tight but it was certainly restraining. He saw the look in her eyes and smiled. It was warm and totally unexpected.

'A marriage has to be based on trust,' he told her seriously, staring deep into her eyes.

Kate looked up, the silence welling up between them as she stared back, unable to comprehend what he meant. Yet her whole heart yearned for it to be a proposal. She nodded with slow understanding, waiting for him to say more.

'So, do you trust me?' he asked, his voice low and soft, his warm breath making clouds in the cold night air.

'Yes, of course. I'll never fail to believe in you again,' Kate replied, deadly serious, her heart beating rapidly, filling her ears with its steady thud.

Sebastian's hands moved gently down the length of her arms till he captured her hands; he raised them to his lips, kissing them tenderly.

'Then will you marry me, Kate?'

She hesitated for a moment, then a slow smile of delight spread across her face, her eyes dancing with unspoken love as she gazed into his eyes. She would tell him about the baby tomorrow, and she knew he would be delighted. But for now. . .

'Yes! Yes! Yes!' she shouted, pulling her hands from his so that she could hug him.

They both fell back on to the soft hay. He locked her in an embrace, his hot lips hungrily seeking hers. 'At last,' he whispered, 'my first and only love. . .'

A years supply of Mills & Boon romances — absolutely free!

Would you like to win a years supply of heartwarming and passionate romances? Well, you can and they're FREE! All you have to do is complete the word puzzle below and send it to us by 29th February 1996. The first 5 correct entries picked out of the bag after that date will win a years supply of Mills & Boon romances (six books every month—worth over £100). What could be easier?

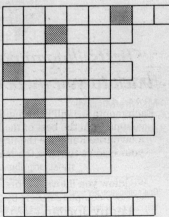

GMWIMSIN

NNSAUT

ACEHB

EMSMUR

ANCOE

DNSA

RTOISTU

THEOL

ATYCH

NSU

MYSTERY DESTINATION

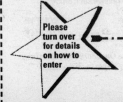

Please turn over for details on how to enter

How to enter

Simply sort out the jumbled letters to make ten words all to do with being on holiday. Enter your answers in the grid, then unscramble the letters in the shaded squares to find out our mystery holiday destination.

After you have completed the word puzzle and found our mystery destination, don't forget to fill in your name and address in the space provided below and return this page in an envelope (you don't need a stamp). Competition ends 29th February 1996.

Mills & Boon Romance Holiday Competition
FREEPOST
P.O. Box 344
Croydon
Surrey
CR9 9EL

Are you a Reader Service Subscriber?   Yes ❑   No ❑

Ms/Mrs/Miss/Mr _____

Address _____

_____

_____ Postcode _____

One application per household.

You may be mailed with other offers from other reputable companies as a result of this application. If you would prefer not to receive such offers, please tick box. ❑

COMP495
B